Priscilla Foster

THE STORY OF A SALEM GIRL

by Dorothy and Thomas Hoobler
in conjunction with Carey-Greenberg Associates
illustrations by Robert Gantt Steele

SILVER BURDETT PRESS
Parsippany, New Jersey

Text © 1997 by Dorothy Hoobler and Thomas Hoobler
Illustrations © 1997 by Robert Gantt Steele
Concept and research by Carey-Greenberg Associates

Published by Silver Burdett Press
A Division of Simon & Schuster
299 Jefferson Road, Parsippany, New Jersey 07054

Designed by JP Design Associates

Manufactured in the United States of America
ISBN 0-382-39640-5 (LSB) 10 9 8 7 6 5 4 3 2 1
ISBN 0-382-39641-3 (PBK) 10 9 8 7 6 5 4 3 2 1

Library of Congress Cataloging-in-Publication Data
Hoobler, Dorothy.
Priscilla Foster: The Story of a Salem Girl/by Dorothy and
Thomas Hoobler and Carey-Greenberg Associates: illustrated by
Robert Gantt Steele.
p. cm.-(Her Story)
Summary: Hannah hears Granny Priss recount her involvement in the
Salem witch trials of 1692 and the terrible consequences that occurred
when Granny Priss, as a young girl, joined Ann Putnam in accusing
many innocent women of being witches.
1. Trials(Witchcraft)–Massachusetts–Salem–Juvenile fiction.
[1. Trials(Witchcraft)–Fiction. 2. Witchcraft–Fiction.
3. Salem(Mass.)–History–Colonial period, ca. 1600-1775–Fiction.]
I. Hoobler, Thomas. II. Steele, Robert Gantt, ill. III. Carey-Greenberg
Associates. IV. Title. V. Series.
PZ7.H76227Pn   1997
[Fic]–dc 20   96-23390   CIP   AC

Photo credits: Photo research: Po-Yee McKenna; 120, Gift of John Cooper
to Harvard College, 1810. © President and Fellows, Harvard College,
Harvard University Art Museums; 121, top: © Brown Brothers, bottom: ©
Culver Pictures, Inc.; 120-121, © Culver Pictures, Inc.; 123, © Culver
Pictures, Inc.

Table of Contents

Chapter 1

"I Was a Witch"

The weather was chilly for September, and all day long a cold rain had fallen. Hannah was surprised when Granny Priss began to look for her cloak.

"You're not going out in this weather, are you?" Hannah asked.

Granny seemed annoyed. "I have to go," she muttered. "It's the day…"

Hannah couldn't hear the rest of the sentence. "The day of what?" she asked.

Granny shook her head. "My boots, where are my boots?"

"They're right under the stairs with the rest of our winter things," Hannah said. She ran to fetch them.

Granny sat on the sofa while Hannah helped her slip on the boots. "I forget too many things nowadays," Granny said. She closed her eyes. "This is the twenty-second of September, isn't it?"

"Yes, that's right. I don't think you should go out, though. Mama will be back soon. Why don't you wait for her?"

"It's the day of the hangings," Granny said. "I have to go. I've gone every year."

"Hangings?" Hannah asked. "No, Granny. You must be thinking of something else. Nobody is being hanged."

"No, that I can't forget. I wish I could. Tie up my boots now."

Hannah wished Mama hadn't left her alone with Granny. "They don't hang people here in Salem anymore, Granny. They take them down to Boston for that."

"They did a long time ago, when I was your age." Granny said. Her sharp blue eyes met Hannah's. "I saw them."

Hannah shivered. She'd never seen a hanging. "What was it... like?"

"Worse than you can imagine," Granny said. "Didn't you ever hear about the Salem witches?"

"Everybody's heard about them, Granny. But it was all a story that people made up, wasn't it?"

Granny frowned. "Made up? No indeed, child. I was one of the witches."

Hannah stared at her. Granny reached out and

took her hand. She still had a strong grip, and pulled herself to her feet.

"What do you mean?" Hannah asked.

"Hmm? I think I'll need a walking stick in this rain."

"Granny, you said you were a witch. What do you mean?"

"I guess nobody ever told you that, did they? It's a shameful story," she said. "But you should know the truth. Because it was lies that caused all the trouble."

Granny found her stick and tapped it on the floor. "Put on your oilskins, then," she told Hannah. "I'll need some help getting up the hill. Come along with me, and I'll tell you all about it. You're old enough to know."

The rain beat down on them as they walked along Essex Street. Smoke rose from the chimneys of the snug little whitewashed houses on either side. Once in a while a horse-drawn carriage passed by on the muddy road. Everything was peaceful and orderly in Salem, just as it had been as long as Hannah could remember.

But Granny Priss's memories went back much farther. Sixty years back. "It was 1692," she told Hannah. "The witch year. I was twelve."

"So you're seventy-two now," Hannah said.

"Well, you needn't show me that you can add and subtract," Granny said crossly. "Being seventy-two is one of the things I'd like to forget."

"I'm sorry."

Granny waved her hand. "Salem was already a pretty big town at that time," she said. "Not as big as Boston, but it had gotten crowded enough for some people to move farther away. They wanted more land to farm on.

"So a group of them settled west of here in what was then called Salem Village. The name is changed today. It's Danvers now. Because after what happened, people wanted to forget all about Salem Village.

"My parents built a house out there, in Salem Village. At that time, it had maybe a hundred houses, but it still wasn't like a real town. The houses were scattered all over. The center of Salem Village just had a tavern and a meetinghouse. A meetinghouse was a Puritan church. Nearly all the people living there were Puritans. You know about them?"

Hannah thought. "A little. They started the Massachusetts Bay Colony, didn't they?"

"That's right. The Puritans had broken off from the Church of England. They thought it wasn't strict enough. And they made so much trouble that the king of England gave them a charter to start a colony in America. He just wanted to get rid of them.

"Well, the Puritans believed that God had specially picked them out. They would set an example to other people by the way they lived. They were going to build a city on a hill, as they called it. That meant everybody else would look up to them.

"But at that time–1692, this was–things were not going so well. Not just in Salem Village, but all over Massachusctts and in England too."

"Granny, what about the witches?"

"Now, don't be in such a rush. This is a long story. I guess they don't teach you young people any history today. But it's important. You have to know about it to understand why people believed in witches."

"You said you were a witch."

"Oh, I was. Just listen for a minute, and we'll get to that. We didn't pass Boston Street yet, did we?"

"Oh, no, that's almost a mile away." Hannah started to worry what Mother would think if she came home to find them gone.

"So we have lots of time," said Granny. "Where was I? You shouldn't interrupt me."

"About things not going so well."

"Yes. Well, there was a revolution in England that overthrew the king."

"Really? I didn't know that."

"So you learned something already. The Puritans weren't too sad, because they didn't like the governor that the old king had put over Massachusetts. They got rid of him and put somebody else in his place.

"And then England got a new king. The Puritans sent one of their leaders to England. His name was Increase Mather. He hoped to persuade the king to appoint a Puritan as the new governor.

"But at the beginning of 1692, Increase Mather was still in England. Nobody knew what would happen to the colony when he returned.

"Meanwhile, some of the Puritan villages up north had been attacked by Indians. The French were helping the Indians, because they wanted to drive the British out of America.

"All these troubles made the Puritans worry. They had always thought that God had intended them to come here. If that was true, why did the colony seem to be in danger? Why did God let the Indians and French burn Puritan villages?"

Granny Priss squeezed Hannah's hand. "You know why?"

Hannah shook her head.

"Because the devil was here, that's why," Granny said.

"The devil?"

"Yes. And as much as the Puritans believed they were blessed, they still feared the devil. He was the source of all trouble. You believe that, don't you?"

"Well...yes."

"But you thought about it before you answered. Because you've never seen the devil. You see, the Puritans thought the devil was right here in Massachusetts. He was roaming around, looking for people to help him in his evil work. If they agreed, he made them witches."

"But you wouldn't have helped the devil, would you, Granny?"

"Well, maybe I did and maybe I didn't. I'll tell you the story and you decide."

Chapter 2

A Coffin in a Glass

It was a hard winter we had in 1692. I thought maybe the snow would stay on the ground forever. We Puritans all believed in hard work, but there wasn't so much to do in the winter. I knitted, mended clothes, cooked, and swept out the house—all the things that women did.

But my mother and my Aunt Lizzie, who lived with us, took care of most of those chores. Father and my two brothers were usually out hunting wild turkeys or ice fishing on the river.

Because I was the youngest child in the Foster family, and the only girl, I was a little spoiled. Most of the time I was allowed to visit my friends, other girls in Salem Village. We'd meet at the house of Reverend Samuel Parris, the local minister. He had a nine-year-old daughter, Elizabeth, and an orphan niece, Abigail, who was my age. Abigail Williams.

Oh, Reverend Parris was a scary man, believe me. Tall and bony, with a face that never smiled. Not all the Puritans were gloomy folk. Most of them were usually cheerful, because they believed they were all going to heaven. But a look from Reverend Parris could make you fear hell.

I don't think Reverend Parris even liked being a minister. He had started out to be a merchant. My father said he owned a ship that carried goods to the West Indies. But it sank in a storm, and he lost all his money. Soon after, he had the call to the ministry, and came to Salem Village.

All Reverend Parris had left were two slaves he had bought on the island of Barbados. Tituba and John Indian. They were married. Tituba took charge of the household, because Mistress Parris was a sickly woman who stayed in her bed most of the time.

The reverend was usually away on church business, so that meant we children could do pretty much as we pleased. Tituba was supposed to watch over us, but when the reverend was gone she joined us in our talk and games.

She didn't much like being a slave. Who would? Tituba sometimes told us she was going to go back to Barbados. We told her if she ran away she'd just be caught and punished. But Tituba said she knew some magic that would help her. Indian magic that she'd learned in Barbados. Now, she could have been put in the stocks or whipped just for saying such things. But we liked Tituba, so we kept it a secret.

That day—the day this all began—Ann Putnam joined us. Ann was only a year older than I was, but she acted like she was the queen of the village already. She was beautiful, oh yes, she was! Young men were already paying attention to her. And Ann was mighty proud of it.

Ann brought along Marcy Lewis, an orphan girl that her family had taken in. Marcy was seventeen, but she was simple-minded. She acted as if she were only six or seven. According to the talk in the village, her parents had been killed by Indians when Marcy was little. She had come home one day to find their bodies. That's what people said. And it had affected her mind.

Ann treated her like a pet of some kind. "Get me that ball of yarn, Marcy," she'd say, and Marcy would go get it. "Go outside and see if it's snowing." Things like that.

Sometimes Ann would tell Marcy to do whatever we told her too. And she would. She just wanted to please everyone. It was cruel, I know. But we never made her do anything bad. Not then, anyway.

This particular day, I remember, it was very dark inside the house. The houses of those times had tiny little windows, to keep the cold out. They were covered with waxed paper, not glass, and even when the sun was shining they didn't let much light in.

The only light came from some logs burning in the fireplace. It was a big two-sided fireplace right in the center of the house. One side of it was on the main room, where we were, and the other on the kitchen. Upstairs, the bedrooms had fireplaces too, but we never went there so we wouldn't disturb Mistress Parris.

We didn't have any toys or games. Reverend Parris wouldn't allow such things in the house. Puritan children were supposed to keep their hands busy with chores. Ann had brought a stuffed cloth ball that we tossed back and forth, but there wasn't much space for anything like that. The ball rolled under a desk that Reverend Parris used for writing his sermons. Ann told Marcy to go fetch it.

Marcy went over and looked, but she couldn't find it. "You're so useless," Ann said. Finally Ann went over herself. She picked up a book that was sitting on the desk.

"Oh, don't touch that," Elizabeth said. "That's Papa's book."

Ann paid no attention, naturally. She brought the book back to where we were sitting and opened it. Holding it close to the fireplace, she studied the title page. We had all learned to read a little, but Ann could read long passages from the Bible. She was smart too. I admit it.

The words in the book were hard even for her. We watched Ann's lips moving slowly as her finger ran across the page. Then she looked up, her eyes shining in the firelight. "It's about witchcraft," she said.

We all jumped. I remember thinking that somebody must have opened the door, because I felt a cold wind blow down my back.

Ann smiled. "Shall I read it?" she asked.

Marcy stuck her fingers in her ears and shook her head. But the rest of us…we were afraid, but we were curious too. Nothing exciting ever happened to us in Salem Village. That was the way life was supposed to be. One day just like the next day, and someday you would die and go to heaven. But this book told about something different. Something exciting.

I think I leaned forward and said, "Just a little bit." Abigail Williams nodded. But little Elizabeth said, "It's an evil book."

She was right, but how could we have known? "It's your father's book," Ann said. "He's the minister. How could it be evil?"

Elizabeth had no answer, so Ann turned the page and began to read.

The book was written by Cotton Mather. He was the son of Increase Mather, the leader of the colony who had gone to England to see the king. Cotton Mather was said to be the smartest man in Massachusetts.

"Go tell mankind," Ann read aloud, "that there are devils and witches in New England." Marcy gave a little squeal, but Ann silenced her with a look, and read on.

Mather wrote about a family in Boston whose children had been possessed by an evil spirit. "They began to shout and roll on the floor with strange fits," Ann read.

"Sometimes they stuck out their tongues down to their chins. Their mouths opened so wide that their jaws were thrown out of joint. The children cried out that someone came in the night to stick them with knives and beat them."

"Oh, stop, please," Elizabeth said. "I can't bear to think about it."

I was frightened too, but I didn't want Ann to stop. I wanted to know what happened to the children. So did Abigail. "Keep going," she said. Marcy had taken her fingers out of her ears, although she was holding them ready to stick back in.

Ann skipped over a few pages. "He tells about all the things they tried to do to help them," she said.

"But nothing worked. Then Mather came to examine the children. They called out the name of a neighbor, an Irish woman who did their laundry. When her house was searched, they found little dolls that looked like the children."

A deep voice came from the shadows behind us. "You stop that now."

Ann slammed the book shut. We all turned around to see Tituba standing in the doorway to the kitchen. She had been listening.

"Bad magic," Tituba said. "Witches use dolls to hurt people they don't like."

Ann was annoyed that Tituba had scared her. "How do you know that?" she asked crossly.

"In the islands," Tituba whispered, "there are many witches. You don't know all the things that witches can do."

"I suppose you know," Ann said.

Tituba nodded. "I know magic, but only good magic."

"Show us, Tituba," Ann said. "I don't believe you." Tituba gave her a hard stare, but Ann didn't drop her eyes.

Then Abigail said, "Yes, show us." She wanted to prove she was as brave as Ann. They looked at me. I was shivering, even though I was standing right next to the fireplace. I nodded. I didn't want to be the scared cat, you see. Ann and Abigail would have made fun of me.

Tituba gave us a sly look that only made me more afraid. "I show you," she said. "But you must promise not to tell."

She went to the kitchen and came back with a glass of water and an egg. She set the glass on the hearth and looked at Ann.

"I see all the young men looking over at you," Tituba said to her. "This will tell you which one you going to marry."

Ann laughed. "Oh, no," she said. "I know who I'm going to marry."

Well, that was a surprise. We all asked her who it was. But Ann wouldn't tell. "I've picked him out," she said, "but it's my secret. No, do something harder, Tituba." She grinned. "Tell us who Marcy is going to marry."

Marcy's eyes opened wide. Everyone could see she'd never thought about getting married. But Ann nudged her. "You're seventeen, Marcy. You ought to be married soon. Don't you want to know who it will be?"

She was so cruel, that Ann. But Marcy was tempted. She put her arms around herself and looked at the rest of us. She wasn't used to being the center of attention.

Ann spoke for her. "Tell her what to do, Tituba," she said. Tituba took Marcy's shaking hand and put an egg into it. "Break it with your fingers," Tituba said. "Not too hard. Just let the white part fall into the glass."

Marcy looked at her and struggled to speak. "What...what will happen?"

Tituba spoke softly. "It will show you the face of the man you will marry."

Marcy hesitated for a long time. But then Ann said, "Go on, Marcy. It won't hurt you."

Marcy broke the egg. We all leaned forward as the white part slipped into the glass of water. The firelight flickered behind it, and we could see it fall to the bottom and then rise again, twisting and changing.

The egg white turned into a long, narrow shape. Then it widened out at the top. It didn't look like a face at all. I tried to think what it reminded me of, but Ann spoke first.

"A coffin," she whispered.

Marcy screamed. It was a terrible noise. And then I realized I was screaming too. So was everybody else.

We couldn't stop. That was the scariest thing about it. I wanted to stop, but there was so much noise that the only way to shut it out was to keep screaming.

The next thing I knew Tituba was slapping us and making us put on our coats. "Get out," she told us. "Go home. Mistress Parris is awake."

I ran all the way.

"But it wasn't over," Granny Priss said. "We had done something that day that I still don't fully understand. We had opened a door for the devil in Salem Village."

Chapter 3
An Evil Hand

When I got home, I felt a terrible chill in my bones. I couldn't stop shivering. I went right to the kitchen, which was the warmest room in the house. Mother and Aunt Lizzie were cooking dinner.

I stood as close to the fireplace as I could. There was a pot of stew hanging over it, and it smelled good. But the flames kept reminding me of the firelight that shone through the glass of water.

"What's the matter, Priss?" Aunt Lizzie asked. "You haven't taken off your coat."

"I'm cold," I said. She came over and felt my forehead. "Oh, child, you've got a fever," she said. "Get yourself right to bed."

I wanted to stay close by the fire. "I'm hungry," I said. "Let me eat first."

"Don't worry, I'll bring you some broth," Mother said. "You know you shouldn't eat a heavy meal when you have a fever."

Aunt Lizzie led me upstairs to the bedroom where she and I slept. My two older brothers had the room across the hall, and my parents' bedroom was at the far end.

She helped me change into my nightshirt. Then I jumped under the heavy quilt on my bed, because I was even colder now. "Don't leave me alone, Aunt Lizzie," I said.

"Now just rest," she said. "Your mother will be up to see you soon."

When she closed the door, I began to be afraid again. Every time I thought about the glass of water, I felt the urge to scream again. But I clamped my hands over my mouth. The story Ann had read kept coming back to me. She hadn't finished, and I didn't know what had happened to the children in Boston. The ones who screamed like we had.

I heard Father and my brothers come home. Their loud voices filled the house, and somehow made me feel safe. I was with my family, I thought, and nothing could hurt me here.

Mother brought me some broth in a cup, and I drank it down in three gulps even though it was piping hot. "Can I have some more?" I asked.

"Not tonight," she said. "If you're feeling better in the morning, I'll fix you a soft-boiled egg with bread. Sleep is what's best for you now."

I didn't want to sleep. But the broth made me feel a little better, and I pulled the quilt tight around me. I dozed off, but woke up again when Aunt Lizzie came upstairs. She gave me a kiss before blowing out the candle and getting into her own bed. It was months before anybody dared to kiss me again.

The next thing I remember, I was screaming again. Just like before, I couldn't stop. It woke up everybody in the house. Suddenly I saw a candle, and then another and another. Mother and Aunt Lizzie and Father were standing there looking down at me. And I still didn't stop yelling, even though I was wide awake.

Aunt Lizzie called through the doorway to James, my older brother. "Get some snow," she said. When he brought it from outside, she pressed it down on my face. It was so cold that it shocked me, and I stopped screaming. I just lay there, breathing hard as if I'd run a mile.

Later on, people made me say that I had dreamed about witches and a tall man in a black hat. That became so real to me that I thought it was true. I don't remember what my nightmare—the first one— was really about. Everything that happened from then on seemed like a nightmare to me.

I didn't sleep any more that night. I had to keep

pinching myself so I wouldn't. In the morning, I was exhausted, but I was relieved to see the daylight come through the little window in our bedroom.

Very early that day, I heard someone knocking at the door of our house. It was Reverend Parris. I recognized his voice, and I tried to listen as he spoke with Mother and Father. Then they all came upstairs.

Reverend Parris walked over to my bed. I pulled the quilt over my face, because I didn't want to look in his dark eyes. I thought he had found out what we did yesterday.

That wasn't it, though. "She has had a fit in the night?" he asked my parents.

"A nightmare," Mother said. "A dream that frightened her."

"Very strange," he said. "My daughter and my niece were troubled in the same way. And so were Ann Putnam and Marcy Lewis. All five of them were together in my house yesterday. I fear they have some illness. We must bring them to Dr. Griggs."

I was relieved to hear that. It just meant that he thought I was sick. Dr. Griggs would give me some syrup or powder, and this would all be over.

But it wasn't. Father put me on the back of his horse for the trip to Dr. Griggs's house. When we went inside, Elizabeth and Abigail were already there. They looked worse than I did. Tears were running down little Elizabeth's face. Abigail gave me a frightened look, and I shook my head. I hoped she knew that meant I hadn't told anything.

Dr. Griggs touched our foreheads and wrists. He asked us what we had eaten yesterday, and if we had any pain. I answered truthfully that I just felt sick.

The door opened, and in walked Mr. Putnam with Ann and Marcy. Marcy was shaking and waving her hands around. She looked as if she didn't know where she was. She could hardly stand up by herself.

Ann was calm, as always. Right away she started to talk to Dr. Griggs. "We had a terrible dream," she said. "Both of us. Somebody was chasing us. They wanted us to do something bad. I told them no, we wouldn't. But then we came to the edge of a forest, and there were Indians there, with hatchets."

Marcy screamed then, and collapsed on the floor. Ann began to scream too, but just before she did, she looked straight at me. I knew she wanted me to do something. Both of them began to roll on the floor.

Then Abigail fell down with them. I wanted to get out of there. I closed my eyes, but I couldn't shut the noise out. And then I began to scream too.

Little Elizabeth cried out, "Stop it! Stop! I can't stand it!" She put her hands over her eyes and suddenly collapsed on the floor.

Dr. Griggs stared at us as if he had never seen

anything like it before. I guess he hadn't. When we girls were all together, we remembered what had happened. I couldn't stop myself, and soon I was rolling around with the others.

Dr. Griggs had a shelf of jars full of herbs and medicines in his office. He took two of them down and mixed the herbs with water. I remember that Father and Mr. Putnam held us down so that he could make us drink it. It tasted terrible. After they let me go, I rolled back down on the floor.

Abigail was jumping up and down now, and nearly trampled on me. Elizabeth tried to run out the door, but her father caught her in his arms. "Lord, help us!" he shouted.

At last the doctor just threw up his hands and turned to Reverend Parris. "There is an evil hand in this," he said.

Of course, the reverend was supposed to be the expert on that, on evil. And he was, oh my, yes. You'll see how he made things worse later on.

In spite of all the noise, I heard what the doctor had said. I thought he suspected what we'd done, and that he thought we were causing the evil. That would mean we'd be punished. So I screamed even louder.

But Ann Putnam came up with something right away. Something clever. I told you she was clever, didn't I? When I heard what she said, I almost laughed. But that would have been a mistake. That's what I thought then. I just wanted to keep my father and everybody else from knowing what we'd done to bring this on.

When Ann stopped screaming, so did the rest of us. Marcy and Elizabeth were still whimpering a bit, but Abigail and I were watching Ann closely.

Ann's body stiffened up like a rod. Her eyes got big and round and rolled back so you couldn't see anything but the whites. Then she called out in this voice—oh, I can hear it now! "Witches," she said. It was like a voice straight out of hell.

Oh, yes. Witches. The rest of us all tried to roll our eyes the way Ann had. It was witches, we cried. Who the witches were didn't matter then. All I knew was, it wasn't us.

Chapter 4

The Names of the Witches

We didn't know it, but the adults in Salem were already worried about witches. Cotton Mather's book was talked about even by those who hadn't read it. Reverend Mather told many other stories of witchcraft besides the one that Ann had started to read aloud. The Puritans in Massachusetts were all ready to believe that God's kingdom had been invaded by witches.

You see, the Puritans couldn't accept the fact that they were ordinary people. Whenever something bad happened to them, they didn't regard it as a natural event. It was a sign that God's plans had been disturbed. And who would do such a thing? The devil, of course—and witches were those who had turned away from God and embraced the devil.

That was why Reverend Parris and the others were ready to believe us when we cried "Witches!"

But then...then they wanted to know who the witches were.

Ann hadn't expected that. But I could see her thinking when Reverend Parris started to question her. It wasn't enough to blame it on Indians that had appeared in a dream. There weren't any Indians in Salem Village. So who had tormented us so cruelly that we screamed?

That was when Ann started to recall her dream more clearly. "I saw a tall man in a black hat," she said. "He came to me and held out a book."

We other four girls screamed. Our terror was real enough, for we thought Ann was about to tell the truth. But no. Ann never came close to the truth ever again.

"He wanted me to write my name in his book," Ann said. "But I wouldn't! I told him to go away."

"Who was this man?" Reverend Parris asked. A good question, for from Ann's description it might have been any man in the colony.

"He didn't say," Ann said. "But I knew...it was Satan."

That set off a new round of screaming. The adults didn't hush us this time. Satan! Just what they were ready to believe. As I recall, Reverend Parris looked almost glad. Satan had shown himself at last, and now Reverend Parris would lead the fight against him.

"Whose names were in his book?" Reverend Parris asked.

Names again, you see. They had to know who was helping Satan. Someone—a real person—must be to blame.

Ann groaned and rolled her eyes again. "I can't read the names."

"We must know," Reverend Parris said. "You don't have to fear them. We will protect you."

Then little Elizabeth shouted a name. She was trying to tell the truth, but wasn't strong enough. "Tituba!" she said.

When Marcy Lewis heard that, she fell to the floor again. I knew she was thinking of the coffin in the glass of water. "Yes!" she screamed. "Tituba!"

At once, Ann took control so that the truth never came out. "Oh!" she cried. "I can see her now! Tituba is standing behind the devil! She has become his servant!"

My father held me by the shoulders. "Priscilla," he said, "is that true? Did you see Tituba in your dream?"

May God help me. I told him yes. I knew it was a lie, but it was Tituba who had shown us the trick with the glass. I hoped they would punish her.

Abigail agreed, but not so eagerly as the rest of us did. She was wondering what Tituba might tell.

Anyway, now they had a name. Right away, everybody who had gathered in Dr. Griggs's office went back to Reverend Parris's house. To find Tituba, the witch.

She was ready for us. Tituba had seen how frightened we were the day before, and she knew that Reverend Parris had taken Elizabeth and Abigail to Dr. Griggs. She figured out that her name would come into the story soon enough.

So she had brought Mistress Parris downstairs and set her in front of the fireplace. Tituba was feeding her some porridge, and looked as innocent as an angel.

Reverend Parris came right to the point. "These girls have told us that you are an agent of Satan," he said.

Tituba gave us a surprised look. Marcy began to scream once more. It didn't take much to get her started. And almost at once, the rest of us were shouting Tituba's name and pointing at her.

Tituba denied everything. Even when Reverend Parris took a broomstick and beat her with it. "Confess!" he shouted. "We know all about you!"

But Tituba just fell to her knees and began to pray aloud. We girls were still making noise, and then Mistress Parris started to scream too. She put her arms out and begged her husband to stop.

Now, Tituba could have told the truth. That would have been bad for us, but it would have put her in even worse trouble. So she refused to confess to anything.

Then something strange happened. Not that things were normal up to this point. But Mr. Putnam stepped forward and asked Ann, "Are there any other witches you can tell us about?"

It was like he was prompting her. And Ann responded quickly. "Oh, yes!" she said, nodding. "I can see them now! Sarah Good and Sarah Osborne!"

I was astonished. Marcy and little Elizabeth screamed all the louder, because it frightened them to think that Tituba wasn't the only witch. But I was pretty sure I hadn't dreamed of other witches.

Ann had picked her targets well. Neither Sarah Good nor Sarah Osborne were well liked by the people of Salem Village. Sarah Good and her husband William were among the poorest people in the village. William earned a meager living as a laborer, but he was so lazy that few people wanted to hire him.

He and Sarah had four children, who dressed in cast-off clothing that Sarah begged from other families. Sarah could often be seen heading for the woods with her basket to gather plants and berries. Rumor had it that she sometimes sneaked cabbages and corn from other people's well-tended gardens. Likely enough, Sarah got blamed for things that raccoons and deer had done.

She had a sharp tongue, though, and let it loose on anyone who accused her. One of those who quarreled most frequently with her was Mr. Putnam. The year before, a shed had burned down on his property. He blamed Sarah, for no other reason than that she was often seen smoking a pipe.

Now, Sarah Osborne was a different case entirely. She was as wealthy—by Salem's standards—as Sarah Good was poor. Her house was one of the best in the village, with oak paneling inside that had been shipped from Boston. That was all due to her first husband, a hard-working man that everyone had respected.

He had died when Sarah was still young, however. So Sarah had brought an indentured laborer from Ireland to run the farm for her. An indentured laborer was only a step up from slavery. He had bound himself to work for four years, and in return Sarah had paid for his ship passage.

Well, when the four years were up, she married him! That was a scandal indeed. Salem Village, like the rest of Massachusetts, was full of gossips. The Puritans were always on watch for misdeeds and sins in others, and they didn't hesitate to point them out. Sarah Osborne and her new husband were the topic of many a talk in the village tavern.

Sarah paid no attention. In fact, she had recently bought a choice piece of land that Mr. Putnam had wanted. Looking back now, I think that was the offense that caused her to be accused of witchcraft.

I was too young then to make such connections. I was still quivering with fear that Tituba would tell what we had done. I thought that Ann had accused the two Sarahs just to muddy the waters a bit.

Much later, I had time to think about it. And I thought it strange that Ann picked out two women that her father particularly disliked.

Chapter 5
The Two Sarahs

Reverend Parris took Tituba and locked her in the woodshed, so that she could do no more harm. As if a witch would let a locked door stop her from mischief!

Meanwhile, Mr. Putnam went right off to Salem Town to find the constable, or sheriff. By nightfall, he had sworn out a complaint against Tituba, Sarah Good, and Sarah Osborne.

My father took me home, and told everybody what had happened. They all looked at me curiously, of course. When I said I was hungry, Mother rushed to bring me a bowl of soup. She and Aunt Lizzie and Father and even my two brothers stood watching as I spooned it down.

Now that I was bewitched, they were all waiting to see if I would show some more signs of it. I could see that they were a little disappointed when I only asked for more soup.

Neighbors stopped by to see me too. The news that there were witches in Salem Village spread rapidly. Ann and Marcy had had another screaming fit on the way home. Mistress Hanks, one of our neighbors, had seen them. "No doubt it was witchcraft," she said. "I've never seen anything like it. Those poor girls."

Again, they all looked at me. And something happened. I didn't really do it on purpose. I just started to remember what I felt like when we looked at the egg in the glass. I could hear Marcy's screams. I closed my eyes, and felt my arms start to jerk back and forth.

And then I was on the floor again, rolling around and around. People were trying to catch me, but I wouldn't let them. Even when Father picked me up, I kept kicking and screaming.

I was bewitched. I knew it then, for certain.

They carried me upstairs and into bed. I remember begging Aunt Lizzie to stay with me. I couldn't bear to be alone.

I drifted in and out of sleep all the rest of that day and night. My nightmare came back, but it was worse this time.

Now I could see them. Just as Ann had said. Sarah Good and Sarah Osborne were poking me with sharp sticks. They held out the book Ann had read from, and wanted me to put my name in it.

"No!" I kept shouting.

The next day, I was weak. I stayed in bed, and kept asking for food. The more Mother brought, the hungrier I got. I kept eating so that I wouldn't fall asleep.

It went on for two days, I think. Then Father stood over my bed and told me I had to get up. The witches had been arrested. I had to go and tell what they had done to me.

Screaming didn't help me now. Aunt Lizzie and Mother got me into my clothes and helped me downstairs. "The other girls are going to be there too," Aunt Lizzie told me. She thought I would be glad to hear that. But it only made me feel worse.

When we arrived at the center of the village, a crowd was waiting. People pointed at me and whispered. I was still afraid, but I felt important too.

Reverend Parris opened the meetinghouse so that everybody could watch the proceedings. Salem Village had no courthouse or jail. And this wasn't really a trial. The trials started much later. This was only a hearing to see if there was enough proof to put the accused witches in jail.

John Hathorne and Jonathan Corwin, two wealthy merchants who came from Salem Town, were the magistrates, or judges. They sat behind a large table at the front of the room.

We five girls sat facing them. The others were already there when I arrived. Ann looked excited, and kept turning around to see the crowd. The other girls hardly glanced at me. Marcy was wringing her hands. She looked as if she wanted to run away. Elizabeth was on the verge of tears, and Abigail just stared silently at the judges.

My stomach churned as I realized I was going to have to tell the story again. Only now there were dozens of people waiting to hear it.

All the benches in the room were filled, and many people were standing as well. The room was more crowded than it usually was on Sundays. The atmosphere was tense, and a low buzz of voices spread through the room.

John Hathorne waved for silence. "A complaint has been made," he said, "against Goodwife Sarah Good, Goodwife Sarah Osborne, and a slave named Tituba. They are charged with tormenting these five girls and others through witchcraft."

And others? I wondered what that meant. Soon enough, I would find out.

The constable led Sarah Good into the room. Standing before the judges, she looked angry and defiant. Her dress was dirty and some of its seams were torn. I heard later that she had tried to escape.

The minister's chair had been turned around so that the prisoner could lean against it. But Sarah stood squarely on her own two feet as John Hathorne read the complaint against her. "What say you?" he asked.

"I scorn it," she replied.

Judge Hathorne stared at her sternly. "Reverend Parris declares that you do not come to meeting on Sundays. Why is that?"

"Look at my clothes!" she replied loudly. "I have nothing fit to wear."

Judge Hathorne then called Ann Putnam's father forward. Mr. Putnam said that last year, Goodwife Good had come to his house to beg for food. "Even though I gave her some," he said, "she showed no gratitude. I heard her muttering a spell as she walked away. The next week, a cow of mine died."

An angry murmur spread through the room.

Mr. Putnam continued, "When I saw her next, I charged her with having witched my cow. She told me she didn't care if all my cows died."

Another man stood up. "She did the same at my house, and the corn withered before harvest."

"She called my son a vile name," shouted a woman from the back of the room. "And he got sick from it."

Others joined in. Judge Hathorne allowed the accusations to go on. Finally he said to Sarah Good, "What is it you say when you go away from a person's house?"

Sarah Good looked around as if searching for a friend. But there were none in that room. "If I must tell, I will," she said. "I say the commandments. I may say my commandments, I hope."

Hathorne nodded. "Then say them now, so we can hear you."

Sarah Good fell silent for a moment. "Thou shalt not..." she began, and then stopped. "The Lord is my..." But she couldn't remember the words.

Ann Putnam broke the silence. "Tell how you come to us at night," she cried. "Tell how you poke us with your broomstick to make us sign the devil's book."

Sarah Good turned and looked at her. At once, Ann held her hands in front of her eyes and screamed. That started Marcy, of course, and then the rest of us. "Take her away!" Ann shouted. "She's hurting us!"

Cries from the crowd added to our screaming. I could hardly hear what Judge Hathorne said next. He called the constable to lead Sarah Good out of the room. She looked around fearfully, and then shouted, "It's not me! Sarah Osborne is the witch who afflicts the children!"

The crowd gasped. People began to shout Sarah Osborne's name. They liked her even less than they did Sarah Good.

When Sarah Osborne was led into the room, she leaned heavily on the constable's arm. She looked ill. Told that she must stand, she grasped the back of the chair. "I am not a witch," she declared before Judge Hathorne said anything.

But he had another witness. Mary Griggs, Dr. Griggs's niece, stepped forward. "Tell us what happened to you the night before last," Judge Hathorne ordered her.

Mary spoke right up. "I live with my uncle," she said. "I saw the bewitched girls when he tried to cure them. After they left, I started to feel as though something evil was in the house."

The meeting room fell silent as everyone leaned forward to listen. I was just as interested as everyone else. I thought witches only bothered the five of us who had been at Reverend Parris's house.

"I went into the kitchen to prepare dinner," Mary said. "I was alone. My uncle was in the front room with Samuel Sibley. Mr. Sibley had a pain in his stomach."

Samuel Sibley stood up in the back of the room. "All this is true," he said.

Mary continued, "Then I heard someone call my name. I turned and saw Goodwife Osborne standing in the fireplace."

"I wasn't there," Sarah Osborne said. "I was home in bed."

"Let her finish," Judge Hathorne said.

"She said she would kill me if I told about the girls," Mary went on. "I screamed, and my uncle and Mr. Sibley came running into the kitchen. They couldn't see her, but I pointed. And Mr. Sibley took a poker from the fireplace and swung it at Goodwife Osborne."

"That's right," Mr. Sibley called out. "And though I couldn't see her, I felt the poker hit her."

"She disappeared then," said Mary.

Judge Hathorne turned to the constable. "Tell us what you saw when you came to arrest Goodwife Osborne."

"Her husband told me she couldn't leave the house because she was ill," the constable replied. "But I made him take me to her. She was in her bedroom, wrapping her arm."

"Her arm was injured?" Judge Hathorne asked.

"It was," said the constable.

"I fell on the stairs," Sarah Osborne protested.

"Show us your arm now," Judge Hathorne said.

Sarah Osborne drew her arm close to her body. "I hurt it," she said. "But I told you, I fell against the stairs."

They made her roll up the sleeve of her dress and take the bandage off. Everybody stood up to see. There it was: a cut with bruises around it.

"That's where I hit her," Samuel Sibley said. No one asked him how he knew where he had hit her if he couldn't see her. Sarah Osborne's protests had no effect. The constable led her away.

When Mary Griggs finished, Ann motioned for her to join us on the bench. As she sat down, Ann put her arms around her. There were six of us now.

Chapter 6

Tituba's Confession

Granny Priss stopped to catch her breath. "Granny," Hannah said. "Did you really think they were witches?"

"Everyone else did," Granny replied. "At the time, all I remember was how relieved I was. Here they had found two witches and I hadn't had to say anything."

Hannah was amazed. "So they took them out and hanged them? Just because people accused them?"

"Not then. They only put them in jail. I told you, the trials were later."

"But didn't anyone say this was wrong?"

"You'll see, you'll see. I must tell you about Tituba first. That was the strangest part of the first hearing."

Tituba had completely changed her story. I don't know why. All I can think of was that Reverend Parris had been talking with her for the past two days. Or beating her. I don't know. But when they brought her into the meetinghouse, she confessed.

Marcy was nervous when Tituba was led in, and I thought she was going to start screaming again. But then I saw Ann reach out and squeeze her hand, and Marcy kept silent. Ann knew. Somehow she knew what Tituba was going to say.

Judge Hathorne hadn't even finished reading the charge against Tituba when she started to confess. She spoke quickly, as if she knew just what she was supposed to say.

"A man came to me while I was in my bedroom," she said. "He showed me pretty things and said I could have them if I served him."

The meeting room fell completely silent. I was terrified, because I still thought Tituba would tell about the things we did with the egg and glass.

But no. She had a much better story than that. "Who was this man?" Judge Hathorne asked Tituba. Everybody thought he was the devil, of course, but Tituba wouldn't say so.

"I never saw him before," she said. "He was tall, with white hair and a black hat. He brought a black dog with him, and other creatures. He told me I must serve them too."

"What other creatures?" Judge Hathorne asked.

Tituba had to think for a moment. "Two cats," she said. "One red, another black, as big as a dog.

When I tried to pray, they scratched me. The man said unless I hurt the girls, the dog and cats would eat me."

"Why did he want you to hurt the girls?" Judge Hathorne asked.

Instead of answering, Tituba turned and looked at us. "I didn't want to hurt you," she said. "It was Sarah Good who made me."

"Sarah Good?" asked Judge Hathorne.

"Yes, her and Sarah Osborne. The man left, but the dog and cats were still there. To watch me. Then Sarah Good came. She had a little bird, a yellow bird, that ate from her fingers."

Tituba held out her hand with the fingers spread wide. "Right there," she said, pointing between her fingers. "The bird drank her blood."

"What about Sarah Osborne?" Hathorne asked.

Tituba nodded her head as if she was glad he had reminded her. "Yes, her too. They made me go with them. They picked me up and we went flying through the air on a stick."

Gasps went through the meetinghouse. I just stared. I couldn't believe what I was hearing.

"Where did you go?"

"To a place way off in the forest. It was a witches' meeting."

"There were others?" Judge Hathorne asked. The room was suddenly silent again. Everyone wanted to hear who the others were.

"Yes," Tituba said. "Nine of them."

A low moan rose up from the crowd. I could hear people muttering, "Nine...nine."

"What were their names?" Hathorne asked. He was very eager, I could see. He was ready to send the constable after anyone Tituba named.

But Tituba shook her head. "They kept their faces from me. I couldn't see who they were. I think one was from Boston. She wore a white silk cloak, pretty."

Judge Hathorne waved his hand impatiently. "What were the witches doing?"

"They cast spells, tried to hurt people they didn't like. They wanted me to join them." She turned to us again. "But I wouldn't do it!"

"But some of these children said you came to them in a dream."

"Sarah Good forced me," Tituba said. "We flew on her stick to find Ann Putnam. Sarah hated Ann.

She was asleep in her bed, and Sarah gave me a knife. She said I should cut off Ann's head."

Ann gave a cry and stood up. She put her hands to her throat and stuck out her tongue. Her body started to shake, and really, I thought that somebody was trying to cut off her head right then.

Then Abigail grabbed her own throat, just like Ann. They were making choking noises. "It's the slave," somebody shouted. "Make her stop!"

Tituba fell to her knees. "I'm not doing it," she cried. "I told the witches I wouldn't do it. Even when they said they would cut off my head. I wouldn't hurt the poor girls."

And then . . . then I couldn't breathe either. I wasn't making it up. It really felt as if something was cutting into my neck. My tongue stuck out, farther and farther as if it was going to jump out of my throat. When I stood up, I realized that Marcy was lying at my feet shrieking.

"Who is tormenting the girls now?" Judge Hathorne shouted at Tituba. She put her hands over her eyes. "I am blind now," she said. "I cannot see."

But Ann could. "It's Sarah Good and Sarah Osborne," she gasped. "They want to kill us!"

I don't remember everything that happened after that. Some people ran out of the meetinghouse to fetch the two Sarahs. They were down at the tavern, being guarded. They had been there all the time we were having our fits in the meetinghouse.

"But then they couldn't have been hurting you," Hannah said.

"Yes, you'd think that now," said Granny. "But you see, at the time people thought that just proved they were witches. They could appear in one place and be somewhere else at the same time. The judges at the trials later on called this spectral evidence. A specter was a kind of spirit, a second body that would let the witches go anywhere."

"Granny, I can't imagine everybody believed that."

"Well, to tell the truth, some didn't. Listen now, and I'll tell you what happened to one of them."

After the hearing, people just wouldn't let us alone. I wanted to talk to Ann. I thought she was the only one who knew why these things were happening. But we were never by ourselves.

We all went over to the tavern. I asked my father to take me home, but he wanted to talk with everyone who had seen the hearing. The tavern was the only other gathering place in Salem Village, and it was full that day. Nathaniel Ingersoll, the tavern-keeper, looked happy. Business had never been so good.

We girls were the center of attention, of course. Ann loved it, but the rest of us were feeling shaky.

I kept rubbing my neck, because it felt sore.

Whenever I did, people pointed and whispered. I started to feel uneasy again. I knew that they were waiting for us to go into one of our fits. And I knew that sooner or later, we would.

Some people got tired of waiting, and left. Ann didn't like that. She was having too much fun, I think. I saw her lean over and whisper something to Marcy. She pointed to a corner of the room, and Marcy's eyes got big and white. She kept shaking her head, and Ann went on whispering.

All at once, Marcy started to scream again. Ann jumped up and shouted, "It's Sarah Good! She's come back for us!" And the whole terrible business started all over again. Abigail, little Elizabeth, and even Mary Griggs—we were all bewitched again.

I was worse now. My body seemed out of control. My tongue was out again, and my arms and legs stuck out stiff, so that I looked like a scarecrow. I couldn't stop myself.

Everybody in the place started running around. Mr. Ingersoll went over to where Ann was pointing and started to hit at the empty air with a spoon. People tried to catch hold of the girls who were rolling on the floor.

And then...somebody laughed. It was a sound so surprising that we almost stopped being bewitched.

The person who laughed was Martha Cory. She hadn't been at the hearing. She happened to walk into the tavern just as the bewitching started. It was the first time she had seen us in one of our spells, and she laughed.

People told her to hush, but she wouldn't. "You fools," she said. "Can't you see these girls are just tricking you?"

Oh, Ann gave her such a terrible look! I shivered to see it. It made me start screaming louder. Ann did even more. She fell down and made her whole body go stiff. The back of her head was banging against the floor. "Witches!" she screamed. "Make them stop!"

Ann was so convincing that nobody listened to Martha Cory. Not one person. But I knew Ann wouldn't forget that she had laughed at us. Martha Cory would pay for it.

Chapter 7

A Day of Fasting and Prayer

Reverend Parris declared that the following Saturday would be a day of fasting and prayer. I didn't look forward to that, let me tell you. We'd had such days before. It meant that everybody would gather in the meetinghouse, praying and listening to Reverend Parris's sermons all day long. Going hungry wasn't the worst of it. The meeting-house didn't have a fireplace, so we'd be shivering in our coats for hours.

Well, it turned out to be a lot more exciting than that. Nobody ever forgot that day of fasting and prayer.

Just about everyone for miles around was there. Even Martha Cory, with her husband, Giles. My whole family went, of course. But I sat up front with the other bewitched girls. Now there were eight of us. Two more girls in the village had dreamed that witches were coming after them. Once the witchcraft started, you see, it spread.

Of course, these girls had seen us at the hearing or at the tavern. That was enough to scare anybody.

But they hadn't named any new witches. And Tituba had said nine, so people in the meetinghouse were looking suspiciously at their neighbors. Maybe there were other witches right there among us. It was just the sort of situation that Ann liked.

Reverend Parris started by reading a passage from the Bible. Then he began to speak of the devil. "The devil has attacked the most innocent members of our congregation," he began.

That meant us. Now of course I knew we weren't completely innocent. But everybody was treating us with such respect, that it was hard to resist. We had become the most important people in the village.

I still had nightmares too. I told myself that I hadn't done anything to cause them. It must be witches doing it. At home everybody kept bringing me food and asking what I wanted. My family had never paid me so much attention before I was bewitched.

Reverend Parris's sermons could last for hours, and I settled back to listen. But after he'd just begun, Ann nudged Marcy, and the both of them started to scream.

I was a little shocked. A prayer service was a solemn occasion. People had been fined just for sleeping during one. The year before, a man had been put in the stocks because he didn't attend a prayer service. Screaming during one was unthinkable.

Except for Ann. And once she started, the rest of us forgot where we were too. Now that there were eight of us, we made quite a racket.

Nobody told us to stop. Reverend Parris just started to speak even louder. I glanced over at Martha Cory. She was shaking her head and whispering something to her husband.

But I was looking in the wrong direction. All at once, Ann pointed up to the rafters of the meeting-house. "I see you, Martha Cory!" she called.

Every eye in the place went up to where she was pointing. It was dark there. The windows were small, and the candles cast only flickering shadows up near the ceiling.

But Ann could see clearly. "Ah! I see you brought your little yellow bird," she cried. "Don't hide it. It's drinking blood from between your fingers, isn't it?"

Oh, she was daring, that Ann. Here the real Martha Cory was sitting right in her place in the meetinghouse. Yet Ann claimed to see her specter looking down on us. She even used the little yellow bird that Tituba had seen first. Of course that was taken as proof that Martha Cory really was a witch.

The other girls, one by one, started to shout they could see Martha Cory too. I strained my eyes, and saw something move up there in the shadows. Even though Martha herself was only a few feet from me, I started to point to the rafters. I really thought I could see her myself.

Then others—grown men and women—started to shout they could see her too. You see how all this happened? Once people started to believe in witches, they became frightened even by shadows.

Martha Cory was stunned. For once, she was speechless. She stood up and turned around, as if to let people see that she was down there, with them. But nobody paid her any attention.

In fact, Martha was one of the most active members of the congregation. But she was a busybody, always accusing others of wrongdoing. She wasn't popular because of that. Nobody was very sorry to see her accused now. When she sat back down in her place, I could see that she had already begun to worry.

Reverend Parris gradually got things under control. He said a prayer, and Ann declared that Martha's specter had disappeared. Even so, I could see people still glancing nervously up toward the roof.

Now it was Abigail Williams's turn to spot a witch. Abigail, you remember, was Reverend Parris's niece. After her parents had died, she had come to live with the Parrises. Reverend Parris frequently reminded her how fortunate she was.

All during the bewitching, I had seen Abigail following Ann's lead. Whatever Ann would do, Abigail imitated it right away. But Abigail wasn't content to be another Marcy. She had seen how much attention people paid to Ann. Abigail wanted that for herself.

Her uncle started to speak again. Looking straight at Martha Cory, he warned the congregation to beware of "the witches among us." Martha poked her husband Giles. I could see she wanted to leave, but he shook his head firmly.

Suddenly Abigail jumped up and started running around the meetinghouse. She flapped her arms, shouting "Whoosh! Whoosh!" It looked like she was trying to fly.

You would think that people would have found that funny. Nobody did. It was clear to everyone, except maybe Martha Cory, that Abigail was bewitched.

"I won't sign!" she shouted. She too had learned from listening to Tituba's confession. "I won't sign your book!"

"Who is it, dear child?" Reverend Parris called from the pulpit. "Tell us who is tormenting you."

Was it Martha who was doing it? That's what I thought. But Abigail was getting ready to name another witch.

Abigail screamed and fell to the floor. Her arms were still flapping. People stood to see her. "Tell!" a woman shouted.

"Oh! Oh! Oh!" Abigail cried. "She has a needle. She's sticking me all over with it."

"Who?" people called.

"I can't see!" Abigail shouted. "She's blinding me!"

"Pray!" Reverend Parris said. "Everyone pray to drive out the witch!" I don't know if anyone but him actually prayed, because everybody was still watching Abigail.

After a few moments, Abigail called, "I can see her now! It's…it's Rebecca Nurse!"

Cries and shouts rose from other places in the meetinghouse. Rebecca Nurse was almost eighty. She was one of the most respected members of the congregation. Everybody knew that she prayed constantly, and never missed a Sunday meeting. This particular day, however, she was home in bed. Illness was one of the few things that excused you from attending a prayer meeting.

Maybe that was why Abigail accused her. Since Rebecca Nurse wasn't there, she couldn't defend herself. Or maybe Abigail really did feel that Rebecca Nurse was bewitching her. I could not tell, nor can I tell you now.

I do know that it was an important moment. It was the first time anyone besides Ann ever named someone as a witch. Tituba and the other girls only mentioned people that Ann had already named.

Now, I believe Ann could have stopped the witchery right then and there. She could have said Abigail was mistaken, and people would have believed her. Perhaps that would have been the end of it.

But after a few seconds, Ann made her decision. She stood and called out, "Yes! I see her too! Rebecca Nurse is here!" She pointed to the rafters again, and yes, many of us saw old Rebecca Nurse lurking there.

Rebecca's sister, Bridget Cloyce, tried to bring people to their senses. She rose from her seat and cried, "How can any of you believe this terrible accusation? You know that my sister is a holy woman who has always lived by the commandments."

We did know that. Or I thought we all did, but later, at Rebecca Nurse's hearing, I learned she had many enemies. At that moment, however, people wavered. They looked at Reverend Parris.

He, of all people, should have shown charity and love. He should have preached a sermon warning us against being too quick to judge others. But Reverend Parris had already made his judgment.

The first words he spoke after Bridget Cloyce's outburst were, "Who knows how many witches there are?" I could hear gasps and moans throughout the meeting hall.

Reverend Parris pointed to us, the girls in the front row. "These poor children have shown us the evil that walks through our village," he said. "Evil that we have not seen, for the devil is a master of deceit. He never works more like the Prince of Darkness than when he looks like an angel of light. Those who serve him may pray and come to meeting, but who knows what they do when we cannot see them?"

Bridget Cloyce could take no more of it. She stood up and stalked out of the church. She was so angry, she slammed the door behind her.

My, I can hear that door slam even now. It was like a crack of thunder. It set all of us girls off, screaming, twisting our bodies into circles. All the time calling,

"Witches! Witches!"

And nobody stopped us. That was what was so amazing to me. Whatever we said, people believed.

Bridget Cloyce herself was accused of witchcraft within a week. Now that Abigail had shown anyone could do it, the names of other witches came tumbling out of the mouths of children, and adults too. From then on, no one was safe.

Chapter 8
Strange Evidence

"Granny," said Hannah, "I want to know something."

"I'm telling you all I can remember. It was a long time ago," Granny Priss said.

"But did people really see witches in the rafters of the meetinghouse? Did you?"

Granny sighed. "I did. I said I did." She paused, and her eyes looked off into the distance, seeing something that was sixty years in the past. "By that time, I thought ... that if I didn't see witches, maybe something was wrong with me. Everything was backward. No one in Salem Village trusted what they saw or even what they thought. That's how twisted our minds became in that terrible year."

One of the strangest things about the witchcraft was how it brought out the worst in people. It was a lie that began all this. Once the lie was told, however, it poisoned the whole village. Old quarrels and resentments, jealousy and fear came bubbling to the surface. The witchcraft became an excuse for the most terrible accusations.

Martha Cory knew that the charge against her was a lie. She told the judges so, but then more lies were piled on that one. The truth became lost. I myself am still not sure what the truth really was.

Martha wasn't arrested until the Tuesday after the day of prayer and fasting. The day before, Ann's father had sworn a complaint against her.

In the meantime, something must have happened inside the Cory house. I don't know what. But at Martha's hearing, the chief witness against her was her husband, Giles.

When the hearing began, the judges asked Reverend Parris to say a prayer. In a loud voice, he asked that the village be cleansed of evil. It was a longer prayer than that, but he left no doubt that evil was right there among us.

Martha Cory stepped forward as if she was ready to put a stop to the whole business. She surprised everyone by asking if she could say a prayer.

Judge Hathorne frowned and shook his head. "We are here to examine you, not to hear your prayers."

"Well, then, I tell you that everything that has been said against me is a lie." There it was. She spoke so firmly that I thought everyone would believe her.

Ann cut off any chance of that. "I saw you," she said. "I saw you on Sunday praying to the devil."

Martha tried to ignore her. "We must not believe what these distracted children say," she told the judges.

"You say that they lie?" asked Judge Hathorne. "Why would they lie?"

Martha hesitated. As I watched, she bit her lip. Then I heard a cry. Ann had bitten her own lip–so hard that blood flowed from it.

Martha turned her head to look at Ann. Ann's head turned in the same direction, and so did Marcy's and Abigail's. The other girls–yes, I as well–started to do anything that Martha did.

I tell you, I felt bewitched again. Whether it was Martha Cory or Ann who had bewitched me, I do not know. I couldn't control myself. When Martha pointed, all of us raised our arms to point as well. When she shifted her feet, we rose in a group and began to dance around. Screaming, by now, of course.

Judge Hathorne commanded Martha to be still. She couldn't. She slammed her hand onto the back of the chair in front of her. All of us did the same. Something made me do it. My hand acted as if someone else was pulling it.

Judge Hathorne brought forward the constable who had arrested Martha. "What did she say to you?" Judge Hathorne asked him.

"She asked if Ann Putnam had told me she prayed to the devil," he said.

Judge Hathorne turned to Martha. "How did you know what Ann had said?"

"My husband Giles told me," she said. "He was in the village when the complaint was sworn."

The judges called Giles Cory to testify. He was almost eighty, older than Martha. I could see he was confused by what was happening. "Were you in the village on Monday?" the judge asked.

Giles looked around the room, as if trying to remember. "She hid my saddle," he said.

"Your saddle?"

"She wouldn't let me go," he replied.

"You old fool!" Martha cried. "That was two weeks ago, when the first hearings were held. I didn't want you to go to the village and get yourself in any trouble."

Miles looked angrily at her. "She calls me names like that," he said. "A wife shouldn't do that."

"Is there anything else your wife does that you find suspicious?" Judge Hathorne asked him.

"She fed the cow, and it got sick," Giles said. "I think she liked the cat better. And sometimes I get up at night and find her saying things in front of the fireplace."

The judges leaned forward, clearly interested in this. "What sorts of things?" Judge Hathorne asked.

"Oh," Giles said, "she talks so low that I can't hear her."

"Could she be praying to the devil?" Judge Hathorne asked.

Giles looked over at his wife. "She says she's praying," he said, "but I can't tell who to. I can't hear her, you see."

That was enough for the judges. As the constables led Martha Cory away, she had one last thing to say. "You can't prove I'm a witch!" she called. That was unwise, for as far as they were concerned, they had proof enough already.

The judges now examined Rebecca Nurse. Though her body was frail, her blue eyes shone with an inner light. My heart sank, for I thought no one would believe this gentle old lady was a witch.

She was hard of hearing, and the judges had to explain twice the charges against her. We made it more difficult by going into our screaming fits again.

Judge Hathorne pointed to Abigail Williams. "This child has declared that you torment her by sticking pins into her body." Just to prove it, Abigail began to howl and declare that Rebecca was doing it again. She held up her hand to prove it. It was true! There were little spots of blood on it.

Rebecca stared at her. "There is another judgment, dear child," she said softly.

I understood what she meant. Someday God would judge us all. At that moment, I understood dimly that what we were doing was wrong. But even then, I could not keep myself from joining in with the others, shouting at her.

The judges called the constable again. "Show us what you found in Goodwife Nurse's house," Judge Hathorne said.

The constable produced several small dolls, dressed as we were—the way all Puritan girls dressed.

Rebecca was puzzled. "I make those dolls to give away to children of the village. Everyone knows that."

Everyone did. But the judges had read Cotton Mather's book. They knew that the woman in Boston had used dolls to bewitch the children.

And now, the parents of children in Salem Village who had received Rebecca Nurse's little gifts came forward.

"Two weeks after my daughter was given the doll, she became ill," said William Lawson. "We feared she would die."

"My little Mary was playing with her doll," testified Margaret Gibbs. "And a spark flew from the fireplace and set her dress aflame."

The milk curdled, the horse hurt its hoof, the chickens failed to lay eggs.... All these and more were among the troubles that befell the people of Salem Village. Now they knew why. They remembered that their children had played with Rebecca Nurse's dolls.

After the evidence had been given, Rebecca spread her arms. We spread ours too. She did not understand what that meant, but the judges did. They asked her if she had anything to say in her defense.

"I can say before my eternal Father," she replied, "that I am innocent, and God will clear my innocence."

She never wavered in her faith. Not even when they took her off to jail.

Chapter 9

The Witch-Fever Spreads

After Martha Cory and Rebecca Nurse were sent to jail, my nightmares grew worse. To my family, of course, that meant that there were more witches in the village.

I tried not to attend the hearing for Bridget Cloyce, the sister of Rebecca Nurse. I pleaded with my parents to allow me to stay home that day. But that just made them more determined to take me. They thought it was the only way I could be cured.

Bridget Cloyce made a bad impression. She was angrier than Martha Cory had been. When we cried out that she was tormenting us, she said, "Oh, you are liars! And God will stop the mouths of liars!"

Judge Hathorne told her firmly, "You are not to speak after this manner in court." As if there were any rules in that court. The judges never stopped any of us from screaming, or anyone else from speaking whenever they felt like it.

Bridget Cloyce declared, "I will speak the truth as long as I live."

But that did not save her.

The witch-fever was a sickness, just like cholera or the flu. It struck without warning. Nobody was immune to it. In the weeks that followed, more and more people were accused of witchcraft. The judges sent almost every one of them to jail. In fact, the jail at Salem Town was so full of witches, that some of them had to be sent to Boston.

Yes, and then the witch-fever spread beyond Salem Village to other towns. I first heard about that when Ann Putnam's father came to our house one morning. Two men I'd never seen before were with him. They were from Topsfield, a few miles north of Salem Town.

Some girls in Topsfield had started to act the same way we had. Screaming without reason, seeing witches in their dreams—oh, yes, Topsfield had its witches too.

The only thing was, the Topsfield girls had not been able to name the witches who were hurting them. So the two men had come to Salem Village to find the girls who could.

Ann, Marcy, and Abigail Williams were ready to go. Little Elizabeth couldn't make the trip. She had become so tormented that Reverend Parris sent her off to relatives in Boston. If only my parents had done the same with me!

But they were proud that I had been chosen for such a task. No matter how much I protested, they insisted I should go to Topsfield. "It is your duty, Priscilla," my father said.

What could I have said? That none of this was real? I didn't know if I believed that myself. My nightmares were real enough. Sitting through all the hearings had convinced me that others had seen witches, even if I hadn't.

So we went. Mr. Putnam drove his wagon with the four of us in the back. Ann and Abigail acted as if we were on a holiday. Marcy was fretful, as always, but if Ann had told her to fly, she would have tried to.

I whispered to Ann, hoping that her father wouldn't hear. "This has got to stop," I said.

"Oh, it will," she replied calmly. "When all the witches are caught."

"But Ann," I said, "maybe they're not witches."

She gave me an odd look. I felt my arms and legs tremble as if I was about to have a fit again. "Of course they're witches, dear Priss," she said. "Who else could be causing this?"

I wasn't ready–not yet–to say that maybe *we* had caused all this. Maybe the egg in the glass had started it. That was too terrible for me to believe.

When we reached Topsfield, a crowd of people greeted us. We were treated like...well, I don't know what! As if we had suddenly become the wisest and best people in the world. As if we'd come to save them from the devil. Which we had, of course.

Ann took charge right away. "Where are the tormented girls?" she asked. The crowd led us to the meeting-house. The girls were kept in there, as if that could keep the witches away. We knew better. You weren't safe anywhere.

There were five, and they hugged and kissed us. I saw that they really were terrified of what had happened to them. They weren't making it up. Oh, no.

One of them, a little girl about nine, would hardly let me go. "Are you going to find the witches?" she asked me. "I'm so afraid. I feel them sticking me with pins and knives every night."

"Yes, yes, we'll find them," I told her. You see how it was? She was so grateful. Like everybody else, she just wanted us to point to the witches.

Ann was hard at work, talking to each of the girls, asking questions. You see, we had never been to Topsfield. We didn't know anybody there. But they wanted us to name the witches, and Ann was finding out names.

Was there anybody they suspected? Did anybody in Topsfield act strange? Who quarreled with their neighbors? Who did people dislike the most? Those were the kinds of questions Ann was asking. Those were the questions that would show her who the witches were.

Finally she was ready. We joined hands with the Topsfield girls and formed a circle. Everybody in the meetinghouse watched and waited. The silence was frightening. I could start to feel again the terror that came upon me in my dreams. So did the Topsfield girls. Soon one of them started to scream, and that set all the rest of us off.

Really, the Topsfield girls didn't put on so great a show as we did. But they learned quickly. Before long, Ann and Abigail had them twisting their bodies into loops and sticking out their tongues. Oh, yes, I did it too. I didn't disappoint anyone.

Ann called out a name. I don't remember what

name it was. "I see her," she cried. "She's one of the witches! She's right here." Then the Topsfield girls saw her too. It was easy for them after Ann told who it was.

That was the way Topsfield found its witches. One name, another name...three in all. I think one was a man. Of course, men could be witches too. Anyone might choose to serve the devil.

The townspeople watching us ran to tell others. Once, Ann named somebody who was in the crowd inside the meetinghouse. That woman cried out and began to protest. It made no difference. Now that she had been named, everybody turned against her.

The next week, the hearings started in Topsfield. We didn't have to go back for them. The same thing happened as in Salem Village. Many of their neighbors came forth to testify against those who were accused of being witches.

It spread all over Massachusetts, I heard. In Salem Town, Billerica, Andover, Boston, and even in settlements in Maine. That year, many, many witches were afoot in the land. I don't remember how many hearings I had to go to.

There was hardly a family that was untouched by the witch-fever. Either someone in the house had been bewitched, or someone else was accused of being a witch. Servants accused their masters, and masters accused their servants.

Some of the people who were accused tried to run away. But there was hardly any place where they were safe. I heard of a wealthy family from Salem Town that went all the way to New York. They found a refuge there. But the constables chased many of the other witches and brought them back.

The constables were allowed to seize the property of those who had been sent to jail. Children whose parents had been accused wandered from house to house, begging for food. A few charitable families took them in, but most people were afraid to. If the parents were witches, they thought, perhaps the children were too.

The witch-fever was all anyone could think about. People started to neglect their fields, and the crops didn't get planted on time. It seemed like everybody spent their days going to the hearings. No matter what happened to the witches, a lot of people in Massachusetts would be hungry the next winter.

In June, more news spread through the colony. Increase Mather had returned from England at last. The king had granted a new charter for the colony and appointed a governor.

Everyone was relieved, for the governor was Sir William Phipps. He was one of us, born in New England. Sir William had gone to sea as a young man, and served in the Royal Navy. Through good luck, he had found a sunken Spanish ship filled with treasure, and the king knighted him for it.

But Sir William was totally unprepared for what he found when he returned to Massachusetts.

Chapter 10

The Trials Begin

Back in England, no one knew anything about the witch-fever that was sweeping through the colony. Increase Mather had left Massachusetts before it started. When he arrived home with Sir William Phipps, they thought that the first problem they would face was the attacks by the French and Indians.

Instead, they found the jails filled with people accused of witchcraft. And more being sent to jail every day but Sunday.

Sir William didn't know what to make of it. He did the only thing that seemed sensible. He appointed a group of the colony's most respected men to a special court. They would hold trials for the accused witches.

Having done that, Sir William gathered a group of soldiers and marched north. He knew how to handle the French and Indians. Probably, he hoped that when he returned, all this witch business would have been dealt with.

It wasn't, of course.

The judges held court in Salem Town. The first person they tried wasn't one of the witches we had discovered. I think Ann was a little upset at that. After all, we had been the first ones to name witches. Ann was eager to testify.

But the court tried a woman named Bridget Bishop, who lived down in Salem Town. It must have seemed like an easy case. She had been suspected of being a witch for a long time. Many of her neighbors were ready to tell about the evil things they suspected her of doing. In fact, we heard that when Bridget Bishop came to trial, she caused a board to come loose from the wall of the meetinghouse.

I never saw that happen, but it was the kind of story people told that year. Witch stories. All I know about Bridget Bishop is that in June, the court sentenced her to death by hanging. And she was.

Well, that should have put a scare into us, don't you think? It was one thing to accuse people of being witches, but another to know that they might die.

It didn't stop anything. By now, the only thing that would satisfy people was for all the witches to be hanged. And they wanted to get right on with it as quickly as possible.

Our turn to testify came soon enough. In July, we all went down to Salem Town for the trials of Rebecca Nurse and Sarah Good. Remember the other Sarah? Sarah Osborne? She had died in jail before they could try her. The jail was an awful place, as I would find out for myself later. I think the judges wanted to hurry up and get to Sarah Good and Rebecca Nurse before they could die too. Jail hadn't been kind to them either.

The trials were held in the Salem Town meetinghouse. It was a much bigger place than the one we had in the village. Even so, it couldn't hold all the people who had shown up to watch the trials.

They came from as far as Boston—men, women, and children. They brought lunches to eat on the town square. It was almost like a fair. There were ministers too, many of them. When I heard someone call out Cotton Mather's name, I turned to look.

He was a stout man with ruddy cheeks, younger than I expected. To make himself look older, he wore a curly white wig. His black coat draped down to his knees, and looked new. Like Ann, he was enjoying himself. People gathered around to hear what he thought of the witchcraft.

We went inside the meetinghouse and were given chairs near the judges' bench up front. Reverend William Stoughton, a minister who had been on the

colony's governing council, was the chief judge. There were four other judges sitting with him. A jury of twelve men had been chosen to decide the fate of the accused witches.

Cotton Mather sat in the front row of the spectators. He watched us closely. I wondered what he would think if he knew his book had been the cause of all this. From what I saw and heard about him later, he wouldn't have been disturbed at all. Witches were as real to him as the trees or the birds.

Judge Stoughton called the court to order. Rebecca Nurse was brought out first. She looked ill and much weaker than the last time we'd seen her. They had to let her sit down, for she couldn't even stand by herself.

Well, we gave Cotton Mather what he had come to see. As soon as Rebecca appeared, we set up such a howl that I thought my ears would burst.

I saw Mather nodding as he watched us. That inspired Ann to throw herself onto the floor, twisting and writhing. Abigail and Marcy were soon right down with her, and me too. Yes.

I've never felt anything like that in all the years since. If you think I was putting on an act, you're wrong. Something evil came over me at those times.

I no longer think the evil came from Rebecca Nurse, or anyone else we accused. Nor from Tituba either. It was evil that had gotten loose in Massachusetts, and for a while, nobody could stop it. But it was real, believe me.

I don't know how long we would have kept on with our fits. The judges didn't try to stop us. But then Cotton Mather came forward and spoke to the judges. I couldn't hear what Reverend Mather said, but they all nodded.

Mather took Rebecca Nurse by the arm and led her to us. "Touch them," he told her.

She looked at him, bewildered. He pointed to Ann, who was curled up backwards like a hoop. "Put your hand on her," Mather repeated, louder this time.

Mather had to hold Rebecca to keep her from falling, but she leaned over and touched Ann's side.

Instantly, Ann stopped screaming. Her body relaxed. I saw her give Mather a smile. She understood what he was doing.

One by one, Mather led Rebecca to the rest of us. When I felt her hand touch me, all the evil seemed to drain out of my body. I didn't want to scream any more.

When Mather was finished, he explained why. "A witch has power only in her spectral body," he told the court. "That is the one she uses for carrying out the devil's work. If her earthly body touches one of those she bewitches, they become cured."

A murmur went through the meetinghouse. Clearly, the fact that Rebecca's touch stopped our fits meant that she must be a witch.

But not everyone believed that. Rebecca's children, all grown men and women, came forward. They gave the court a petition signed by twenty-seven of Rebecca's neighbors. Brave people! They declared that Rebecca was a saintly woman who never did harm to anyone in her life.

Judge Stoughton read the petition to the jury. "This has been brought forward by the accused witch's children," he said. "You should consider their natural feelings toward their mother."

Judge Stoughton went over the other testimony against Rebecca. Among other things, he described the way she had tormented Abigail by sticking her with pins.

One of Rebecca's children stepped forward. "I was at the hearing when that happened," she said. "I saw this child pull a pin from her dress and stick herself."

Abigail stiffened. The members of the jury looked at her. "It's a lie," Abigail cried. "It was she who did it."

Then the dolls Rebecca had made were displayed. "What harm could there be in these?" Rebecca's daughter declared. "I played with such dolls myself when I was a child."

"Yet many people from Salem Village testified that the dolls caused harm," Judge Stoughton pointed out. "Some of them are here." He called people forward to retell their stories.

Still, the members of the jury seemed impressed by what Rebecca's children had said. Ann was becoming restless. I wondered if she might go into one of her fits again.

Just as the judges were about to send the jury out, the constables brought in the next accused witch. As it happened, it wasn't Sarah Good. It was Deliverance Hobbs, another woman from our village. She wasn't one of the witches we had accused. A servant girl had named her.

But Rebecca Nurse turned to see what was happening. When she saw Goodwife Hobbs, she cried, "You have her too? Why she is one of us!"

I don't know what she meant by that. Since Rebecca had been in jail for months, she must not have heard about all the others who had been accused. But the judges would draw meaning from Rebecca's words before long.

The jury went outside the meeting hall to consider the case against Rebecca. Later on, I went to several more of these trials. It usually didn't take long for the jurors to make up their minds.

This time it did. No one else left the room, and there was a low buzz of conversation. Rebecca's children gathered around her, quietly assuring her that she would soon be free. Some of them glared at us from time to time.

Ann and Abigail whispered furiously to each other. The business about the pins had bothered them. I knew that Ann would much rather have started the trials with Sarah Good, who had no one to testify on her behalf.

I felt sick. Not the way I had been earlier, when one of my fits started coming on. I remember hoping that the jury would find Rebecca not guilty. Maybe that would end the witch-fever. I didn't want to start screaming and twitching again. But I knew I would, as long as there were witches around.

Finally Judge Stoughton sent someone to urge the jurors to make up their minds. They filed back inside then. The room hushed as everyone waited to hear their verdict.

The leader of the jury stood. "We find the accused, Rebecca Nurse," he said, "not guilty of the charge of witchcraft."

Oh! What a cry went up in that room! It seemed to me as if all the people had been bewitched all at once. The Nurse family, of course, was crying out with joy. But almost everyone else seemed outraged by the verdict.

Two of the judges rose and began to shout at the jury. Ann, Abigail, and Marcy started to scream and stick out their tongues again. I think I was the only person in the room not screaming. I felt relief. Now it was over, I thought.

Finally Judge Stoughton brought order back to the court. He addressed the jury. "I have no wish to impose on you," he said. "But I wonder if you have considered fully the words Rebecca Nurse spoke at the end of her trial. When she saw another accused witch enter the court, she said, 'She is one of us.'"

The jurors were flustered. The head juror looked at Rebecca Nurse and asked her, "What did you mean by those words?"

Rebecca didn't reply. I don't think she even remembered what she had said. She knew she had been declared not guilty, and thought the trial was over. She was hard of hearing too, and might not have heard his question. But because she didn't answer…they thought she recognized Goodwife Hobbs as another witch.

Judge Stoughton sent the jury back to reconsider. In less than a minute they returned. "We have changed our verdict to guilty," the foreman announced.

This time, only the Nurse family protested. Judge Stoughton paid no attention to them. After a few words with the other judges, he sentenced Rebecca Nurse to hang.

Chapter 11
The Hangings

"Granny, that was so unfair," Hannah said. "How could the judges have done such a thing?"

Granny Priss shook her head. "I don't know," she said. "Everyone but Rebecca's family seemed glad. When the people waiting outside heard that she had been declared guilty, they cheered."

"But she was innocent, wasn't she?"

"Oh, yes, child, of course she was. I know that now. But you see, the witch-fever had infected everyone. They feared the devil so much that they would have done anything to drive him out of Massachusetts. And the only way they could do that...was to hang witches."

"This is Boston Street, Granny," Hannah said.

"Oh, yes. We must turn up here. This is the way the wagons went when they took the witches to be hanged."

Hannah looked up the steep hill. The gray cobblestones were slick from the rain. "I don't think you should try to

walk up the hill, Granny," she said. "Let's go home."

"No," Granny Priss said firmly. "I must. I have come every year. I want them to forgive me."

The trial of Sarah Good went more quickly. There was hardly anything to it. Once Rebecca Nurse had been convicted, the jurors understood what their duty was supposed to be. I think only one man came forward during the trial to defend Sarah Good. Not long afterward, Ann discovered that he was a witch too.

As for me, my dreams grew worse. I knew exactly who appeared to me now, however. It was Rebecca Nurse. She stood over my bed every night and said, "There is another judgment, dear child."

I screamed and screamed. When my Aunt Lizzie held me in her arms, she asked who was tormenting me. I told her it was Rebecca, and she said, "She'll soon be hanged, Priscilla. Don't worry. Then she can't hurt you any more."

I knew better than to believe that. I wanted to tell Aunt Lizzie exactly how the witch-fever got started, but I was afraid to. When I did tell, later on...but we'll get to that.

My parents decided it would be good for me to go see the witches being hanged. That was how the Puritans thought. People were always punished in public, whether they were put in the stocks or whipped or hanged. It would be a lesson to others. In my case, it was supposed to cure me from being bewitched.

Just about everybody in Salem Village went down to Salem Town for the hangings. Of course a lot of other people came too. Such a crowd! Really, I think it was about the most exciting thing in people's lives.

There were five witches being hanged that day. July 19, it was. Rebecca Nurse, Sarah Good, and three other women that I hadn't known. They were brought up the hill in wagons. In those days, this was called Gallows Hill. People lined up along Boston Street to watch them pass.

No one showed any charity toward them. Boys tossed clods of mud at the wagons and the adults cried out, "Your time has come, witches! You'll meet the devil today!"

The Sunday before this, Reverend Parris had stood in the meetinghouse and declared that Rebecca and Sarah were no longer members of the church. That wouldn't have mattered to Sarah, but for Rebecca, it would have meant that her soul would go to hell.

I don't know if anyone told her, because all her relatives had stopped coming to church meetings. Bridget Cloyce, Rebecca's sister, was still in jail, and so was another of their sisters, Mary Esty. People whispered that the whole family must be witches. The Nurses had started to carry muskets with them whenever they came to the village, which wasn't often.

Reverend Parris followed the witches up the hill in his own wagon, bringing Abigail, Marcy, and Ann. When they saw me, they invited me to join them. I remember how proud my parents were.

I forced myself to get into Reverend Parris's wagon. I thought maybe I could talk to Ann and Abigail. Tell them about my dreams. I don't know...I was hoping that they could say something that would stop the hangings.

I was foolish to think that. Ann waved gaily to the people along the street. I remember that the wagon carrying the witches got stuck in a rut. The horses strained to pull it forward. At once, Ann stood up and cried, "The devil wants to save them!"

"I see him!" Abigail shouted, trying to outdo Ann as usual.

But Ann had the last word. She beckoned to the crowd. "Good people!" she cried. "Lend your backs to lay the devil flat."

A mob of onlookers rushed forward and started to push the witches' wagon. It rolled forward, headed up the hill to the gallows tree.

I looked at Ann's face, and then at Abigail's. They glowed with triumph. It was as if a fire burned within their hearts. I turned away. I knew that my own heart was full of doubt, but I was helpless.

"That's the tree," Granny Priss said.

Hannah shivered. It was a big oak tree, standing alone at the top of the hill. Its leaves had started to turn red now that autumn was here. The rain made the leaves shiny, like blood.

The jailers had chained the arms of the condemned prisoners behind their backs. The first one to hang was Sarah Good, I think because she was protesting so loudly. As the executioners dragged her toward the tree, she cursed us all.

Nicholas Noyes, a minister from Salem Town, stepped forward. "You have been proven to be a servant of Satan," he told her. "You stand before us justly condemned."

Sarah shouted right back at him. "You are a liar," she cried. "I am no more a witch than you are a wizard, and if you take away my life, God will give you blood to drink."

Her speech shocked the crowd. If anything, it proved how evil she was. Some years later, Nicholas Noyes died from an illness that caused him to cough up blood. He choked to death on it, people said. And they remembered Sarah Good's last words.

The executioner hauled Sarah Good up the ladder to the branch that held the noose. After fastening the noose tightly around Sarah's neck, he pushed her off. It took her a few minutes to die, but it seemed much longer. Her body and legs thrashed about. Then her face gradually darkened. I had to turn away from her. I couldn't stand to look. All around me, however, people had their eyes turned upward, fascinated by the sight.

The other witches must have watched it too. I have often wondered what they thought at that moment. None of the other four women struggled like Sarah Good. Two climbed the ladder without help, as if they were eager to die.

The executioner saved Rebecca Nurse for the last. How cruel that was! She couldn't walk at all by now, and the executioner had to carry her up the ladder. I could hear her praying. At the last moment, just before the noose was slipped over her head, she asked the executioner to let her speak.

Rebecca's words were far worse than Sarah Good's. "I pray that God will one day give proof of my innocence," she said. "And I pray that He will forgive all who have accused me."

Mercifully, her neck broke as she fell. The crowd gave a sigh as they saw Rebecca was dead. Were they disappointed? Relieved? Or did a twinge of fear pass through people's minds? I knew only one thing: This must stop. I could not send anyone else to be hanged.

Granny wandered to the edge of the rocky cliff on the far side of the hill. Hannah ran after her, afraid that Granny might slip and fall.

"Down there," Granny said, pointing. "You see the cracks between the rocks? That's where they threw the bodies after cutting them down. Witches couldn't be buried in a

cemetery, in holy ground. They tossed them down there, and hoped that no one would remember them.

"I heard that the Nurse family came in the night to recover their mother's body. They buried her somewhere else, and never revealed the place. I can't pray at her grave, so I tell myself that she had forgiven me as she died. But I knew that I must do more if I was ever to forgive myself."

Chapter 12
The Truth

Who could I tell? That was the question I asked myself all the way back to Salem Village. Reverend Parris certainly would not listen to me. Every Sunday, he proclaimed how important it was to be on guard against the witches. People found new ones almost every day.

My parents were so proud of what I had done that I was afraid to tell them. All the judges lived in Boston or Salem Town, so I couldn't go to them.

That night, I decided that Aunt Lizzie was the only person I could trust with my secret. When we were getting ready for bed, I told her that something weighed deeply on my heart.

"Why, Priss," she said. "You should be relieved now that those who tormented you so cruelly have been punished."

"I have done something terrible," I said.

"Something so bad that I don't know if I can ever be forgiven."

She shook her head. "Child, you are young and innocent. That is why the witches chose you as one of their victims."

"No," I said. My voice was shaking, but I was determined to go on. "I am not innocent. I fear that I have sent those who really are innocent to their deaths."

I closed my eyes to avoid the startled look she gave me. I told the story of the afternoon at Reverend Parris's house when Ann read from the book. How we put the egg in the glass, and why we started screaming.

"That was what started the witch-fever, Aunt Lizzie," I said. "It was us."

She shook her head and put her arms around me. "No, dear Priss," she said. "That cannot be. Many, many nights I have heard you screaming in your sleep, shouting the names of witches who were in this very room. I myself have seen them."

"You saw them?" I was astonished.

"Yes, of course. I prayed and they went away. I saw Martha Cory on the roof-beam in the meeting-house too. Everybody did. And consider all the other people who have come forward to tell of the witches' evil deeds."

"But they—" I didn't know what to say.

"No, Priss," she said. "if only you and the other girls had seen witches, people might have doubted you. But so many, many people have seen them that there can be no doubt."

"They said those things because of the way we acted," I insisted.

"Many others have been afflicted," Aunt Lizzie pointed out. She took me by the shoulders and made me look at her. "I advise you not to repeat to anyone else what you have told me, Priss. It can only cause confusion."

That night, I kept myself awake by pinching myself and clenching my hand around a pin. It was the only way to ward off the dreams I feared. Even so, I could not keep the face of Rebecca Nurse out of my mind.

The next day, I couldn't eat either. When my mother insisted that I have a little vegetable broth, I threw it up. I sipped water only after my mouth grew so dry that I had to.

That went on for a week. I dozed off every now and then, but as soon as the dreams began I woke up and began pinching myself. I began to lose weight and looked so terrible that Aunt Lizzie made me stay in bed. "You have to rest, Priss," she said. "On Tuesday you must go to Salem Town again."

"Why?" I asked.

"For the trial of Martha Cory."

"I can't," I said. "I won't. I won't testify against anyone else."

Aunt Lizzie rubbed my forehead. "I know this has been hard on you, Priss," she said. "But you must summon the courage to fight the evil that afflicts you. So that others will not have to suffer."

I shook my head. I knew what the evil was, but Aunt Lizzie wouldn't believe me.

Then I realized what I had to do. The only place I could do it was at a trial. The judges would have to believe me. At last, I slept. And no dreams disturbed my rest.

The next morning I ate everything that my mother put in front of me. She was so happy. I tried not to imagine what she would think of me by the end of the day.

"You don't have to go with me," I told my father as he went to hitch our horse to the wagon. "You should stay here and work in the fields. The weeds are taking over."

"No, Priss," he replied. "It's more important that we all go to support you."

I'm sure he meant it. But our plot of ground, like everyone else's, went untended that summer. Catching witches was more important than anything else.

When we reached Salem Town the crowds had gathered again. We made our way to the meeting-house, and I joined Ann, Marcy, and Abigail once more. For the last time, I hoped.

When the constables brought in Martha Cory, the howls and contortions began again. This time, I struggled not to join in. It was hard. I gripped the seat of my chair to keep from falling off. "It's not real," I kept telling myself. "There aren't any witches." When I wanted to scream, I pressed my hands to my mouth. Even so, I was shaking all over.

The judges ordered Martha to touch us, to stop our fits. Martha's stay in jail had not dimmed her spirit. She approached us with rage in her eyes.

Martha did more than touch us. She slapped Ann directly across the face. Cries of outrage swept through the room. Ann did come out of her fit, though. I could see a red mark on her cheek. Ann seemed not to care. She gave Martha a look of triumph.

Martha was not deterred. She slapped Marcy just as hard, and then Abigail. When she stepped toward me, I stood up and turned to the judges.

"She doesn't have to slap me!" I cried out. "She's not a witch!" Suddenly I realized that the entire room was silent. Everyone was staring at me. I struggled not to go into a fit. I had to speak the truth.

"We learned about witches from a book," I told them. My voice sounded very loud. "And then we put an egg into a glass. It was at Reverend Parris's house. We were playing, that's all. But then—"

"A book!" It was Ann's voice. I turned to find her pointing at me. "She signed the devil's book! Oh, Priscilla, how could you do that?"

"No, it's not true," I said frantically. Already I could see people's faces changing as they looked at me. "It wasn't the devil's book," I cried. "It was Reverend Parris's book!"

"O, what a lie!" shouted Abigail. "Priscilla, I see you clearly now! You've joined the devil's side!" She gave a shriek and started hopping around, clutching at her side. "She's stabbing me!" she cried out. "Make her stop!"

Poor Marcy wasn't as quick-witted as Ann and Abigail. She looked back and forth at us, and then did the only thing she could think of. She fell to the floor, her body as stiff as a plank, and began to scream.

"Make her touch them!" Ann called out. "Priscilla is bewitching them. She's a witch!"

"And so I was," Granny Priss said. "I deserved to be one, after all. I had called so many others witches."

"But you had told the judges the truth this time," Hannah said.

"They wouldn't listen to anything I said. They forced me to touch Abigail and Marcy. When their fits stopped, that was enough proof to have me arrested."

"Oh, Granny," said Hannah. "Nobody ever told me about this."

"Of course not," Granny Priss said. "Even now, people want to forget all about the witch year." She took one last look over the hill. "Let's go home now," she said. "I've said my prayers. I asked them to forgive me."

"But what happened?" Hannah asked. "Did they send you to jail? Why didn't they...?"

"Hang me?" Granny shook her head. "That was just luck. I'll tell you the rest of the story as we walk."

Chapter 13

In Jail

The constable took me out of the meetinghouse and bound my hands with rope. My parents and Aunt Lizzie followed us. I can't tell you how awful it felt to see the looks they gave me. They were ashamed. It was a terrible thing, shameful, to have a witch in the family.

Aunt Lizzie came to speak to me when the constable put me into the prisoners' cart. "I'll bring you food, Priss," she whispered. "Pray for forgiveness. You can still save yourself."

I sat in the cart for a long time. My hands grew numb from the rope. Inside the meetinghouse, the trial was still going on. Finally, the constable put two others into the cart. The last people I wanted to see, Martha Cory and her husband, Giles.

As things turned out, the judges didn't sentence Martha Cory that day. Ann and Abigail had tried their best, but the judges wanted to hear the testimony of her husband. And he wouldn't speak.

Giles didn't realize, at the hearing months earlier, that they would put his wife in jail. Since then he had wandered around the village asking where she was. When it finally dawned on him what had happened, he refused to speak to anyone. The constables had to carry him into court for the trial. And no matter what questions the judges asked, Giles responded with silence. So they sent both him and Martha back to jail until he changed his mind.

Martha, as might be expected, had plenty to say to me on the trip to jail. My, what a tongue that woman had! I understood why her husband had testified against her earlier.

I deserved everything she said, of course. When I tried to explain to her what really had happened, she wouldn't believe me either. She thought we girls had gotten together and planned to accuse people we didn't like of being witches.

As we arrived at the jail, however, I got a surprise. "Of course," Martha told me, "even though I'm falsely accused, there really are witches."

I couldn't believe my ears. "You?" I said, "You believe in witches too?"

"There are many of them in jail here," she replied. "They'll tell you so themselves."

It was true. The jail had an effect on people's minds. Although most of us were not kept in chains, our surroundings were a constant torment. All the women and girls were kept in one large room with bare stone walls. It was always dark, because there were only one or two tiny windows near the ceiling.

Some women had to be chained, because they had gone mad. They would have injured themselves or someone else. All day long, their screams and moans echoed off the walls.

And yes, there were several women who openly declared that they were witches. I recognized one. She was Dorcas Parker, one of the witches Ann had discovered in Topsfield. Like Sarah Good, she had been an outcast. Now she told everyone that she had sold herself to the devil. "He will help me, you'll see," the poor woman proclaimed. "I will never hang, no. I will fly out of here at night and kill all those who accused me."

With all the noise, I didn't realize that someone had come up behind me. I jumped as I heard Tituba's voice.

She was surprised to see me. "How come you be here?" she asked.

"Ann and Abigail accused me of being a witch," I said.

"Oh, yes, them bad," she said nodding. "You know what you should have done? Tell on them."

I could see her grin. "I tried," I said. "I told all about the book and the glass with the egg in it. But no one would listen."

"Not that," Tituba said. "Simple, you say they are the witches, not you. Everybody believe that."

"I don't think so," I replied.

"Oh, yes. See all the people in here. Many good people. Who would have thought them witches? Look over there." She pointed to what looked like a small pile of rags in a corner. But it moved, and I could hear a child crying underneath.

"That the daughter of Sarah Good," Tituba told me. "She only four years old, but somebody call her witch and now she here too." Tituba whispered in my ear. "She don't know her mother hanged."

Tituba tapped me on the shoulder. "Best thing for

you now," she said. "Confess."

"Confess? You mean admit I'm a witch?"

She nodded. "Tell them you was a witch, but now you repent. They let you out then."

I shook my head. "That's what you did, wasn't it? Why are you still here?"

"I go out sometimes," Tituba said.

I cringed. I thought she was going to tell me she flew through the air at night. But Tituba wasn't that foolish.

"They bring me out for trials," Tituba explained. "I say what they want me to say. I see who they think is witch and I tell yes."

"But that's wrong!"

She shrugged. "You tell me that wrong, but you name me as a witch, remember?"

I hung my head, ashamed.

"All this is wrong," Tituba continued. "If I don't confess, they hang me. For me, jail is better than working for Reverend Parris. He whips me, but nobody does that here. Every week, my husband John brings me something to eat. You got somebody to do that? Food very bad that they give you here."

"My aunt said she'd bring me some," I told her.

"You tell her you will confess," Tituba said. "Then they let you out."

Just as she'd said, the food was really very bad.

We were given only a bowl of thin gruel and a cup of dirty water twice a day. The prisoners whose relatives and friends brought them food sometimes shared it with the others.

The nights were the worst part of being in jail. People kept screaming. If you lay down on the stone floor, rats came out and scampered over you. I tried to sleep leaning against the wall. Even when I did sleep, I had nightmares. Only now, there was no one to comfort me.

When Aunt Lizzie did come with food, she gave me the same advice Tituba had. "You have to confess that you're a witch, Priscilla," she said. "Some people who have done that are being let out of jail."

"But that doesn't make any sense," I told her.

"The judges ask the confessed witches to tell about the other witches," Aunt Lizzie said. "And you've already done that."

I shook my head. "No," I said. "I won't do it any more. I'd rather stay here."

So I did. Another month went by, and more witches were condemned to death. Four men and a woman. The jailers told us about their hangings, taunting us that we would be next.

I was afraid. I kept thinking about what it would be like to have the noose slipped over my head. After a while, it was all I could think about.

The judges were moving slowly, considering how many witches were now in jail. Dozens in Salem Town, where I was, and more in Boston. Even so, I knew that someday my turn would come. No one would testify in my behalf. Except maybe my family, but that wouldn't help me.

I thought and thought during the weeks I spent there. I accused myself, and said that I deserved to be in jail. But I stopped at the thought that I was really a witch. I knew I wasn't.

But the longer I stayed in jail, the more afraid I became. One day, when Aunt Lizzie was visiting, I gave up. I didn't want to die. I told Aunt Lizzie that I would confess.

"No, Granny," Hannah said. "You didn't."

Granny nodded. "I did. You see," she said, "I realized that earlier I had accused people falsely. But everybody believed me. Then I told the truth, and nobody believed that. So, I thought, I might as well accuse myself of being a witch if that was what it took to get free."

"But you didn't accuse anybody else, did you?" Hannah asked.

"No," Granny said. "I got out of that. But I had to go to another hanging."

Chapter 14

A Confessed Witch

Aunt Lizzie arranged for me to have a hearing so that I could confess. It was easier than I thought it would be. It was held in Salem Town, not the village, so only my family was there. Ann and the others weren't needed, since I was confessing.

I followed Tituba's advice, up to a point. I admitted that I had been a witch but said I had been confused and tormented. My parents and Aunt Lizzie testified about my dreams and the terrible tortures I had been through. I said that I had never signed the devil's book and declared that I would have no more to do with witchcraft. I was sincere about that.

When the judges asked me about other witches, I said that I had seen some but they had blinded me. I couldn't tell who they were.

One judge was a minister from Boston. He seemed kinder than most of the other judges I'd seen.

He asked me if I'd ever tormented anyone when I was a witch. I told him no. "Did you know you were a witch before someone accused you?" he asked.

His questions made the other judges uncomfortable. But anyhow, they set me free. They reminded me that if I recalled the names of any witches, I had to testify against them.

I was relieved, of course, but going back to Salem Village was hard. Whenever I went outside, people pointed at me and whispered. I could hear them saying, "That's one of the witches."

I was careful to avoid meeting Ann and Abigail. I heard they were angry that I had been let out of jail. Fortunately for me, they were kept busy testifying at the trials in Salem Town.

In September, I had to go too. Martha Cory was being tried again. This time, the judges thought they had found a way to make her husband speak. Old Giles was carried into the meetinghouse yard and tied to the ground. Everybody crowded around to watch as the constables began to place heavy rocks on top of him. This was supposed to squeeze out the truth.

With each rock, the constables asked Giles if he would testify. Old as he was, Giles had plenty of strength. I stood at the back of the crowd, but I saw the size of the rocks they used. It took four men just to carry one of them.

There was a roar from the front of the crowd, and I thought Giles must have agreed to testify. But then, what he really said spread through the crowd from person to person. Giles had gasped, "More weight."

That was all he said. At last, the rocks crushed him to death. After people wandered off, all I could see was a huge pile of rocks. Giles was underneath. But he never said a word against his wife.

Even so, the judges condemned Martha to be hanged. She and seven others. On September 22, sixty years ago.

Once more, everybody in Salem Village went to see the hangings. I pleaded with my parents not to take me. But of course I had to go. I had confessed to being a witch, and if I didn't attend the hangings, it would seem I really hadn't repented.

In a way, I'm glad I did. It was still a terrible thing to see, but something happened that caused people to start to change their minds.

One of the people sentenced to be hanged was George Burroughs. He had been the minister in our village a few years earlier. He left because some of the villagers, including Ann Putnam's father, had criticized his sermons.

Burroughs went to Maine and started a farm.

Imagine how surprised he must have been when the constables arrived and told him he had been accused of witchcraft. By Ann Putnam, naturally.

One of the odd things people said that summer was that witches could not recite the Lord's Prayer. It was one sure way to tell that they were witches.

George Burroughs knew that. When the executioner put the rope around his neck, Burroughs asked to say a few words. Given permission, he began to say, "Our Father, which art in Heaven...."

Everyone watching, who had been jeering and calling him a witch a moment before, fell silent. Burroughs spoke loudly. I'm sure I wouldn't have had his courage, with death waiting for me. We all listened as he said every word of the Lord's Prayer, right to the end.

Even so, he got no mercy. The executioner pushed him off the ladder anyway. I don't think Burroughs really expected to be saved. Like Rebecca Nurse, he wanted to prove that he wasn't a witch.

Martha Cory, waiting in the cart with the other witches, saw what Burroughs had done. She too went to her death with the Lord's Prayer on her lips.

George Burroughs and Martha Cory didn't save themselves that day, but I am convinced that they saved many others. Standing in the crowd, I could hear people start to ask questions. Questions that should have been asked long before.

If the witches were really servants of the devil, how could they pray and praise God?

Was it right to condemn them? Was it right? For the first time that year, people asked that question. They began to have doubts.

Not everybody, of course. Cotton Mather was at the execution. Hearing the murmuring in the crowd, he came forward and gave a speech. "The devil may often appear as an angel of light," he said. "Do not be deceived by his tricks."

Others were not so sure. One of the judges who had condemned people to death resigned from the court.

A few weeks later, Sir William Phipps returned from battling the French and Indians. He found that the trials had not stopped new witches from appearing. I even heard that in Boston, Sir William's own wife had been accused of witchcraft.

That cleared Sir William's head. He ordered all executions stopped until he could consult with a council of ministers.

Stories began to spread about the witches who had already been hanged. Some of them appeared to people in dreams, claiming their innocence. That was disturbing news. It meant that the witches were not silenced by hanging, as we had been told. Of course, it could also mean they hadn't been witches at all.

Finally, when harvest time came, the yield was very sparse. People suddenly realized that there would be little to eat that winter. All the fuss over the witches had only brought disaster on the colony. And perhaps that meant that God did not approve.

I tried to stay at home as much as I could. The trials were still going on, but I was never called to testify. For the first time, though, juries began to find some people not guilty. This time, they did not reverse their verdicts.

One day in November, my father came home with news he had heard at the village tavern. Sir William had pardoned the latest group of witches to be condemned.

"What reason did he give?" I asked.

Father shook his head. "I don't know," he said. He gave me a long look. I knew that there were many questions he wanted to ask me. I knew that he remembered what my part in the witch-fever had been.

Instead, he just said, "Perhaps it's over now. It would be better not to speak of what has happened." And we didn't. From that day on, the word "witch" was not spoken in our house. The subject was never discussed.

"Wait, Granny," Hannah said. "You mean they never asked you what had really caused your fits?"

"Never," Granny said firmly. "It was too painful a thing to recall."

"That's hard to believe," Hannah said.

"That was the way it ended in most places," Granny told her. "People just stopped accusing witches. No one spoke about it. No one wanted to."

I remember the last time I ever heard a person accused of being a witch.

Late in November, I went to the village with my father. It was a cold day, and we stopped in the tavern for a glass of hot cider.

I saw Abigail sitting by the fireplace all by herself. I think she had come in because she was lonely. Her cousin Elizabeth had not returned to her family, and Ann Putnam hadn't shown her face in the village ever since the pardons.

Abigail looked up when my father and I came in. I thought she wanted to say something to me. But Father pulled me away to a table at the other end of the room.

The tavern was busy that day. As we sipped our cider, people stopped by to say hello to my father. They nodded in my direction, as if to say, "We're glad you've recovered." But they never mentioned it. Here I was, a confessed witch, but nothing was said about that.

A young girl, no more than ten, came into the tavern. She was one of the children of the accused witches who were still in jail. She wore only a thin dress, too little for the cold day. She went from table to table, asking for coins.

People were generous, and someone bought her a glass of cider and a roll. That bothered Abigail. Suddenly she stood up and pointed at the girl. "Watch out!" she cried. "She's brought the devil in with her!"

Silence fell over the tavern. One by one, people turned their backs on Abigail. I saw her face get red, and then she began to scream.

Right away, Nathaniel Ingersoll, the tavern-keeper, came over. He took Abigail by the shoulder and roughly pushed her right out the door. Everybody returned to their conversations. Ingersoll even gave the little beggar-girl a bowl of hot soup.

Chapter 15

Why I'm Telling You

Hannah and Granny Priss were almost home now. They walked slower on the trip back, because Granny often had to stop to rest. It was getting dark by the time they reached the street where their house was. Oil lamps began to shine inside the other windows along the street.

Hannah saw that Granny was tired. Still, she couldn't resist asking her more questions.

"What did they do with all the witches in jail, Granny?"

"Yes, that was a problem," Granny remembered. "At the end of 1692, Sir William dismissed the judges of the special court. There were no more trials after that.

"But Cotton Mather and some of the other ministers still insisted that the witchcraft was real. It wasn't until the next spring that Sir William announced a general pardon for all the witches in jail. Even so, some of them didn't get out right away."

"Why not?"

"Because if you were in jail, even if you were innocent, you had to pay the jailers for the time you spent there. They charged for your meals and for keeping you locked up. My parents had to pay for me when I was let out earlier."

"That's terrible."

"Yes, Hannah. Well, at least they weren't hanged. Reverend Parris refused to pay to get Tituba out of jail. He still believed she was a witch. Somebody else paid for her, though. People took up collections to free those who couldn't afford it. Tituba ran off with her husband, just as she said she would. Nobody ever saw her again."

"What about the little girl?" Hannah asked. "Sarah Good's daughter."

"Oh, yes," Granny replied. "Somebody paid for her too. She was never right in the head afterward, however. That was true of Marcy, too. She never recovered, and died a few years later. I thought about the coffin in the glass when they buried her."

"What happened to Ann and Abigail? Weren't they ever punished?"

"Not exactly. The next year, the villagers decided they wanted a new minister. Someone who had no connection with the witch trials. Reverend Parris made them pay him a lot of money to go, but they finally did it. He took Abigail with him. I never heard what happened to them."

"But Ann was the leader of it all, wasn't she?"

"Yes, I guess so. People did realize that. You know, none of the young men in Salem Village ever did court her. They were afraid of her. I don't know which one she had picked out the day we started the witch-fever. But she never married anybody."

Granny smiled. "I guess no one in the village would have married me, either. But a few years later my parents moved down to Salem Town to get away from all the bad memories. That's where I met your grandfather. He was a sailor, you see. He didn't know much about what went on during the witch year.

"Somebody told him once that I had been a witch. Warned him. He just said, 'Well, then she can cast a spell to keep me safe while I'm at sea.' He sometimes joked about it. I never told him the real story."

"You didn't? Ever?"

"No. I told your mother when she was about your age. And now I'm telling you."

"Why is that?"

"Because...I've always been afraid that it might happen again."

Timeline

This timeline shows the major events of the Salem witch trials.

January–February 1692

In Salem Village, Massachusetts, Elizabeth Parris, Abigail Williams, Ann Putnam, and Marcy Lewis began to speak incoherently and shriek for no apparent reason. They accuse Tituba, Sarah Good, and Sarah Osborne of bewitching them.

March 1–5

John Hathorne and Jonathan Corwin serve as judges at an examination of the three accused witches. Tituba confesses to witchcraft. All three are sent to prison.

June

Sir William Phipps appoints a court to try the witches. William Stoughton is the chief judge. The first person tried is Bridget Bishop, who is sentenced to death and hanged.

1692

February

Other girls in the neighborhood, including Ann Putnam, accuse Tituba, Sarah Good, and Sarah Osborne of bewitching them.

March 21–24

Marcy Lewis, Rebecca Nurse and Sarah Good's four-year-old daughter, Dorcas, are accused of witchcraft and sent to prison.

June 29

Five more accused witches are convicted and sentenced to death. Rebecca Nurse is one of them.

April

At least twenty-three more women and men are accused and sent to jail.

May 14

Sir William Phipps, newly appointed governor of Massachusetts, returns from England with Increase Mather, one of the colony's leaders.

William Stoughton

July 19

The five condemned witches are hanged on Gallows Hill in Salem Town.

August

Six more accused witches, four men and two women, are sentenced to death. One woman is reprieved because she is pregnant. The others are hanged.

Sir William Phipps

1693

May 1693

Sir William Phipps orders the release of all accused witches.

1706

October 12

Sir William Phipps stops further executions for witchcraft.

September

Fifteen more accused witches are sentenced to death.

September 19

Giles Cory is pressed to death because he refuses to testify.

September 22

Eight of the condemned witches are hanged.

1706

Ann Putnam, then about twenty-seven years old, writes an apology for causing the deaths of innocent people. It is read aloud in the Salem Village meetinghouse by the new minister. Ann says the events of 1692 were caused by a "great delusion of Satan."

Increase Mather

The True Story

The story you have read here is fiction. Yet all of the events are based on fact. Except for Priscilla Foster and her family, all of the characters in this story were real people. Some names were changed to avoid confusion. You can look at the timeline in the back of this book to see what actually happened.

The complete story of the witch trials is very complicated. We have changed it somewhat in writing our book. Most of the testimony in the witch trials comes from historical records. But we have combined several trials into the few described in this story.

Cotton Mather really did write a book called *Memorable Providences* in 1789 that may have played a part in starting the widespread accusations of witches. Mather did not testify at any of the trials, but he suggested the "touch test" to the judges. Mather did, however, speak to the crowd at the hanging of George Burroughs, just as we describe.

Many people have written about the Salem witch trials in the three centuries since 1692. Two books that we found valuable were *Delusion of Satan*, by Frances Hill, and *The Devil in Massachusetts*, by

Marion L. Starkey. You can probably find both of them in your local library.

Nathaniel Hawthorne, the famous nineteenth-century author of such novels as *The Scarlet Letter*, also wrote a short story about the witch trials. Nathaniel Hawthorne was a descendant of John Hathorne, one of the judges at the witch trials. Nathaniel changed the spelling of his last name (adding the "w") because he was ashamed of his ancestor's actions.

Cotton Mather